Jinzo Naruse

A Modern Paul in Japan

An Account of the Life and Work of the Rev. Paul Sawayama

Jinzo Naruse

A Modern Paul in Japan
An Account of the Life and Work of the Rev. Paul Sawayama

ISBN/EAN: 9783337170400

Printed in Europe, USA, Canada, Australia, Japan

Cover: Foto ©Raphael Reischuk / pixelio.de

More available books at **www.hansebooks.com**

PAUL SAWAYAMA.

A MODERN PAUL IN JAPAN

.

An Account

OF THE LIFE AND WORK OF THE
REV. PAUL SAWAYAMA

BY

JINZO NARUSE

WITH AN INTRODUCTION
BY
REV. ALEXANDER McKENZIE, D.D.

———

"No thought, no word, no act of man ever dies. They are as immortal as his own soul. Somewhere in this world he will meet their fruits in part; somewhere in future life he will meet their gathered harvest."

———

BOSTON AND CHICAGO

Congregational Sunday-School and Publishing Society

Dedicated to

MY AMERICAN FRIENDS

WHO OUT OF LOVE FOR JAPAN

HAVE ENCOURAGED ME IN

MY LIFE WORK.

PREFACE.

REV. DR. NEESIMA and the Rev. Paul Sawayama were the two great captains of Christ, in Japan. Both died on the battlefield, fighting the good fight. Dr. Neesima having laid the foundation of Christian education, the Japanese people respect and love him as the Father of Education. Rev. Paul Sawayama having laid the corner stone of the Independent Christian Church, the people respect and love him as the Father of their Faith.

It has seemed possible, having come into close relationship with the choice spirit of our loved brother, Paul Sawayama, in both companionship and Christian work, in our native land, that it may be my own special province and privilege to try so to bring before all students of our native characteristics his admirable traits of character and sweet spirit. By so doing, perhaps, a new view may come to light of the possibilities wrapped up in the hearts of the many Japanese Christians who are earnestly desirous of living up to the pattern of the meek and lowly Jesus Christ.

It is also hoped to open up the deeper side of the Japanese character, to show the enthusiasm of the young Christians there, their power of self-reliance, and the eagerness and strugglings of the young women for improvement.

I wish here to express my hearty gratitude to my friend, Rev. C. S. Patton, Pastor of the Congregational Church of Auburn, Maine, companionship with whom at Andover Theological Seminary facilitated my study of the English language, and to whom I am much indebted for the kind assistance and encouragement which enabled me to accomplish this work.

J. N.

August. 1893.

CONTENTS.

INTRODUCTION

THE Christian world has become specially interested in the educational work in Japan, through the valuable services of Dr. Neesima. This interest will be enlarged by the memoir of Paul Sawayama, which is now presented by Mr. Naruse. Probably a clearer idea of the nature of this work and of the circumstances under which it must be carried on can be obtained from memoirs of this character than in any other way, while the personal narrative is vivid and instructive. Facts are more convincing and abiding than theories, and those which belong to the effort of a man whose life is given in them are of singular force. I am confident that the readers of Mr. Naruse's interesting pages will be profited by his story of a useful career. The high endeavor of which he writes must commend itself to all who care for Japan and who see in the education of women a large and assured hope of the advance of the country in the Christian knowledge which must elevate the people of that land, as of any land. It is greatly to be desired that the author of this narrative may be enabled to fulfill the high purposes with which he has labored here and with which he returns to his own people. So far as this book shall further this desire it will be a noble extension of Mr. Sawayama's influence and of the work which controlled his life.

ALEXANDER McKENZIE.

THE FIRST CHURCH IN CAMBRIDGE,
    September 15, 1893.

A MODERN PAUL IN JAPAN

CHAPTER I.

SAWAYAMA'S YOUTH.

MR. SAWAYAMA and the writer were born contemporaneously in the same town and were brought up in similar families, belonging in the same class, samurai,[1] under the same prince. We thus received the same influences from

[1] Up to twenty-five years ago there existed four social distinctions among the people. The first of all these classes was samurai, which may be translated knights. Next to this came the class of farmers. The reason why they were placed next in importance to the samurai was that they provided all necessary things for living. Next to the farmers came the class of artisans or carpenters, and the last of all came the merchants or tradesmen, who were regarded as the lowest and most useless class of people, because their aim was that of making money. The sentiment of the people in regard to money may be seen in the following:—

"The wise man loves wisdom, but the foolish man loves riches.

"The foolish man, although *possessing riches,* is like a flower under frost — decaying; while the wise man, although in poverty, is like a lotus *springing up* from the mud."

the same surroundings, the same instruction and discipline from the same masters at school, Mr. Sawayama being a pupil in my father's private school.

I would like to give the reader a correct impression of Mr. Sawayama's childhood. As the particular events which belong to it are naturally somewhat indistinct in my memory, the picture which I wish to present may perhaps be best drawn if I state some recollections of my own childhood. In the mirror of this the reader may discern how Mr. Sawayama's life began, and may appreciate how it developed into that beautiful and noble Christian character which made it a power in Japanese life.

Mr. Sawayama was born in the Province of Chōshū, under the shadow of the magnificent mountain Idsumi, in the seventeenth year before the Japanese Revolutionary War. The writer was born ten years later in the same village.

My earliest recollection is that of the

flower gardens and groves which surrounded my home and the hedge of evergreens which enclosed the yard. My mother has often told me how, when I began to creep, I was entrusted to servants who allowed me to creep about in the garden. The servants at noon on one warm day left their small charge to amuse himself and all went in to their dinner. The most inviting amusement seemed to be to creep toward a pond which was a few yards from the gate. Once at the edge of this pond, the natural thing was to creep still farther. A man coming along a moment later, found a baby floating upon the water. He hastened to save it, but it was already breathless.

The servants ran out in great fright, and having built a fire and warmed the body and having swung their neglected charge rapidly in the air to revive him, they waited in great anxiety the appearance of my father. They dreaded his anger, for he might well be angry over the danger into which their neglect had brought his only son and heir.

But when my father returned from the office of the prince, he was very calm and self-possessed.   He did not speak a single word of anger or even of reproach.   For at such a time the mind of the samurai must not be shaken up by any emotion. He was trained to stand bravely before any and all troubles which might come. He must not allow himself to change complexion, though sorrow, poverty, or even death should fall to his lot.

"While there are no strivings of pleasure, anger, sorrow, or joy, the mind may be said to be in the state of equilibrium. When these feelings are aroused, if they act in their due degree, there ensues what may be called the state of harmony. This equilibrium is the great root from which all that is good in life springs ; and this is the path which all should pursue." This philosophy the samurai obeyed vigorously.   I remember, when my mother

and my aunt and my younger brother
died, how I, as a child, could not control
myself but wept bitterly ; but my father
preserved his tranquility of mind perfectly and I never saw a tear so much as
start to his eye. In one instance, indeed,
he came near losing his envied harmony
for a moment ; but he only came near
losing it and only for a moment. A few
days before his own death, while he was
enfeebled by a very severe illness, the sad
report came to him that my younger
brother had died suddenly at a remote
place. I was at his side when the news
came and I saw him cover his face for
an instant with the comforter ; but when
he looked up again I saw no trace of
tears.

As to the education of our childhood,
it consisted chiefly in learning to read and
write, in hearing lectures, making poems,
calculating numbers, drawing, and fencing. In the early morning, before break-
fast, we were taught reading ; in the day-

time we listened to lectures, and in the evening we were taught calculation.

It was a very great task to commit to memory the several thousand characters which, imported from China, were used in writing Japanese, though we had the Japanese original alphabet which consists of forty-six letters.[1] And it was a very hard task for such small children (I began to go to school when I was five) to wake so early at all seasons of the year and in the most severe winter weather to enter the schoolroom with no fire in it. And in the summer it was a very *sleepy* task, for we were not allowed to sleep early in the evening, but at that time were compelled to receive our instruction in mathematics.

Sometimes we were made to go to school barefoot in the snow or over the hoar frost. These things which may seem like hard treatment — and there were

In Japanese one letter stands for one syllable, while in Chinese, one character stands for a word.

many such things in a boy's education —
were regarded as no less important a part
in education than were the studies which
we pursued. For by such treatment the
parents of the samurai class sought to
develop in their children what they call
" *Yamato-damashi*," the Japanese spirit,
that is, the spirit of self-denial, of self-
sacrifice for prince and country. They
sought to develop also what they call
harakiri, or, the spirit of suicide. This
word *harakiri* means literally the cutting
of the abdomen. The motive of parents
in teaching the spirit of *harakiri* was to
produce that bravery which would make
one willing to die for others or for the
sake of any good cause. It was a shame-
ful thing if a samurai was not brave
enough to commit *harakiri ;* for by his
cowardice he would show that he was not
able to die for the sake of righteousness
or for his prince or country. Thus it
came to be regarded as a great disgrace
to die by the sword of another or to be

captured in battle. *Harakiri* was the sign of that heroism which was the special characteristic of the samurai.

Among many instances which I might give of this spirit of *harakiri* which prevailed among the samurai, I will give only one, which came under my personal knowledge : —

My teacher's brother, when under the influence of wine, almost unconsciously uttered some words which were thought to imply rebellion. Trouble ensued, and at last he was ordered to commit *harakiri*. He prepared a place for the execution at his own home. Several officers, his brother and near relatives were present. He took a short knife and cut his stomach from side to side, then thrust his knife into his throat and fell dead.

If any man of the samurai class had committed any crime, it was a great disgrace for him to receive his execution at the hands of another. Or if he were overcome in battle, the only honorable course was for him to prevent his capture by taking his own life. The cultivation of this spirit was an essential part of the samurai's education.[1]

This ideal of strictness which the samurai taught his children he strove to inculcate, not only by instilling the principles upon which it rested, but by his own example. We had many forms of propriety which were enforced by very stringent rules, — an elaborate and finished system of politeness. For instance, there was the rule for sitting down on the mat in the true Japanese fashion. It was not usual to practice this every day and on all occasions, for it was very tiresome, if not absolutely painful, to sit in such a cramped position a long time, while reading, or writing, or speaking, or doing business at the office. So the lower class

---

[1] For this reason the Japanese called the two swords, carried by the samurai from childhood to old age, *Yamato-Damashii* — Japanese spirit. One of them was long, and this served for fighting and protection; while the other one was short, which served for *harakiri*. The wearing of the two swords stopped in 1868, after the revolution which destroyed the feudal system.

of the samurai often allowed this rule to go unnoticed in their private rooms. But my father never lost the extreme strictness of his manners, in this or in any particular, even in his most private rooms. My mother has told me how he would never put his feet out against the hearth in the coldest winter weather, lest he should set the example of carelessness before his children. Thus he never ate candy or fruits at the improper time; he never went to the theatre, because he thought that these things contained strong temptations for children, and he would set no example except of the strictest propriety. But he drank wine and smoked tobacco, for the Japanese never considered these as bad habits for mature people. "Wine is the king of all medicine," they said.

It was the custom of parents also to encourage their children in their studies by telling them stories of enthusiastic students and what happened to them.

A very common story was that of an earnest student who one day became so interested in his study that he did not notice that a shower had begun to fall until the corn which he was drying in the sunshine was washed away by the flood. Another story was that of the poor boy who, being unable to buy oil by which to study, studied in the summer evenings by the light of the fireflies which he caught, and in the winter by the reflection of the snow. There was also the account of the self-denying student who put his head through the noose in a rope which he suspended from the ceiling; and when his head dropped forward as he fell into a doze, he was suddenly awakened, and went on with his study.

The morality of the time was a somewhat peculiar one, which came from an alloy of the Japanese Shintoism and the Confucianism and Buddhism which were imported from China.

The first duty was the religious one — to obey the decrees of heaven, and to serve the spirits of ancestors.[1] The most familiar obligation was that of obeying the decrees of heaven : " What heaven has conferred is called the nature ; an accordance with this nature is called the path of duty; the regulation of this path is called instruction."

The next duty was that of the "*go-rin*," or the duty of the five relations. These five relations were, first, the relation between master or prince and servant; second, that between father and son ; third, that between man and wife ; fourth, that between brethren ; fifth, that between friends.

Thus, fidelity, loyalty, and patriotism were the highest virtues; and the Japanese people have many great examples of

[1] The way of serving ancestors was to offer water or incense or flowers or other things at the altar of the spirits of the ancestors in the home, and tablets in the Buddhist's temple and at the graves in the cemetery. They believed that they could communicate with the spirits of ancestors by worshiping and offering such things as the above.

these virtues. I myself never had the
experience of military service in behalf
of the prince, for I was too small at the
time when such service was needed by
him. But I remember clearly the desire
which I had to become a soldier during
the closing scenes of the war. I was
then about twelve years old. I asked
my father's permission. He was silent.
After I had waited several days for him
to speak to me, I understood by his continued silence that he would not allow
me to go the battle field.

If my father's silence, in this instance
just mentioned, should seem strange to
Americans, as my observation would lead
me to suppose it might, let me explain
that in Japan the scholar or prudent man
does not speak much. He controls his
family by a silent authority. Even yet
a peculiar tendency toward soberness, or
almost toward severity of expression and
feeling, is noticeable among the Japanese.
" Fine words and an insinuating appear-

ance are seldom associated with true virtue," they often say.

Filial piety was a virtue next in importance to loyalty. " Filial piety is the root of all virtues." The child or youth must be studious, must practice the truth, must take care of his health, must avoid dangers, not so much for his own sake as because he owes it to his parents. When I was a boy my great delight was to see the happiness of my parents over such progress as I made in my studies; or to bring to them for their approval the results of a hunting or fishing expedition. But according to my own feeling, and my own case is merely a typical one, my father was too stern, and my mother was, perhaps, too affectionate. I never had what Americans call " fun " with my father,— never joked with him; but I often conversed, or even played with my mother; and while of course I did love my father and did respect my mother, yet it seems a much more natural statement of the case to say that I respected my father, but loved my mother. I even had a voice against my mother's commands sometimes, and occasionally I would disobey her; but in all my life I never disobeyed my father, nor can I remember a single instance in which I remonstrated by even so much as a word or sign against any command of his.

One sentiment which from childhood we were taught to repeat often, was this: " What you do not want done to yourself do not do it to others." My father was very strict in requiring my obedience to this rule. One day (I must have been about nine years old), a boy friend and I began to quarrel. At length we came to an open fight which continued for almost two hours, sometimes one and sometimes the other appearing to have the better of it. I was almost tired out when my friend offered to submit. He was so sorry over the trouble that he went to my father to make his confession to him.

My father came to me immediately, and, after scolding me for my fault in the quarrel, punished me severely. He tied me to a stake with a cord holding my hands behind my back, and wrapped my body around with a coarse mat of straw. I remained two hours in this condition. I must confess that I had a little feeling against my father for this; and after I was set at liberty, instead of going into my own home I went to that of my uncle which was near by. But I soon repented and went home and took dinner with my father. He treated me with especial kindness that night and my dissatisfaction soon vanished.

It was very common when I was a boy for boys to fight by standing at some little distance from each other and throwing stones. In one of these battles I was hit upon the upper lip. When I went home to my dinner my lip was badly swollen and was very painful. I told nobody about the matter, and though my father must have noticed the condition of my face he seemed willing to let me take my swollen lip as my punishment and said nothing.

I was punished only twice by my father. One occasion was that which I have already described; on the other, my father beat me about the head with a short stick because I was stupid in my study.

Our chief negative commandments were: do not lie; do not steal; do not covet. And the training which we received in the keeping of these was constant and emphatic. I remember my father sending me on an errand to a store at a distance of a mile or more. I made my purchase, paid the money, received the change and returned home. When I gave the change to my father he noticed that the storekeeper had given me back one rin (one tenth of a cent) too much. I was ordered to take the one rin back immediately. The impression was thus forced through my legs into my mind that my father was exceedingly careful over what seemed like a very little thing.

The following case will also show the reader to what a degree the hatred of dishonesty was carried. A schoolmate of Mr. Sawayama's had stolen a stick of Japanese ink from his friend's box. He was found out. All the students gathered at once around a pond; they threw the thief into the water; many threw stones at him; and if he climbed up to the shore they pushed him into the water again and again until the poor fellow was almost dead; then he was dismissed from the school.

We were taught that if we spoke a lie we would receive punishment from God in this world, and in the next world our tongues would be cut out of our mouths. When I was ten years old I went one day up a sacred mountain to worship a god. I was told that if anyone had told a lie in the past time he would be caught by the bellrope of the temple and would not be able to loose himself from it. I was frightened and examined my heart pretty carefully.

I will say in a word how we were taught to examine our hearts and to keep our consciences active. When I was tempted to sin in the darkness, I repeated these words: "Heaven knows, and I know, and earth knows; I cannot escape from the net of heaven; there is nothing more visible than what is secret, and nothing more manifest than what is minute; therefore the superior man is watchful over himself when he is alone."

Such precepts as the following were helpful in our efforts to examine ourselves, and repent of our faults: "I daily examine myself on three points; whether in transacting business for others I may have been unfaithful; whether in intercourse with friends I may have been insincere; whether I have mastered and practiced the instruction of my teachers."

"When you have faults, do not fear to abandon them." "I have faults — to refuse to reform them, *this* should be pronounced the greatest fault."

The first duty of the day was to worship the gods. In the morning I used to worship the god of heaven and earth, the god of water, the god of the mountain, the god of the clan. This I did standing outside the house. Then coming in I worshiped the spirits of my ancestors and the god of the household. We had not only gods of agriculture, medicine, etc., but a god to care for each particular member of a man's body; such as a god of eyes, a god of teeth, etc. In all, we believed in several thousand gods.

But we regarded the God of heaven as the king of all the gods and the ruler of all things. But of course the idea of God was very dim; we conceived of the invisible world of gods or spirits as an organized society, like human society. As a king has many officers, so there are

many gods of every kind and degree, all
doing the bidding and performing the
work of the God of heaven. We thought
of the spirits of these Gods as scattered
throughout nature, and as having their
individual dwelling-places in various objects, such as the sun, the moon, the
temple, the idol.

The chief influence of my early religious life came from the death of my
mother, which occurred when I was six
years old. After I lost my mother my
first serious question was: Is there a
heaven in the future, or will the human
life be blotted out as the light of a candle
disappears? One day, having pondered
this question a great deal, I proposed it
to a woman who answered me: "No;
there are no such things in the future;
heaven and hell are all in this world. If
you are in misery, you are in hell, and if
you are happy, that is heaven."

I was not satisfied with this reply. I
could not be content to think that I

should not see my mother again; nor did it seem to me that on such a hypothesis my own life was other than a vain thing, though I should learn ever so much and store up for myself all the writers of the Japanese ideal of life. My anxiety over this problem led me often to inquire of scholars, or of the priests of Shintoism or Buddhism; and though almost all of them believed in heaven and hell, I was never entirely satisfied with their answer.

When I had reached the age of about thirteen, the western sciences, history, philosophy, and mathematics were imported into my native town. The new truths which came to me through these channels made a deep impression upon me. I saw the foolishness of worshiping idols and abandoned it immediately. Having as yet nothing in its stead I was entirely nonreligious for a long time. But having read the story of creation in the Western History, I tried one evening to worship the heavenly God; but my

heart and my mind were full of doubts
and fears. I had this hope, however;
that probably the Western nations had
discovered the true religion, since they
had found out so many truths concerning
philosophy and science. Soon I came
upon my great opportunity to hear about
Christianity; for Mr. Sawayama had
returned from America with the Christian faith. As soon as I heard of his
return I called upon him and asked him
the many questions which had so long
been troubling me. He answered me
very earnestly, clearly, and wisely. My
eyes were opened at once to a new world,
and I became a Christian.

From this time to the time of his death
I was working almost constantly with Mr.
Sawayama. I seem to myself to know his
life almost as well as I know my own.

CHAPTER II.

SAWAYAMA'S CONVERSION.

MR. SAWAYAMA had from his childhood been fond of study, and had at different times attended the best schools in his native province. In 1868, when he had reached the age of seventeen, a great crisis occurred in Japanese affairs. In the revolution against *Bakufu*[1] Mr. Sawayama's province was attacked by the *Bakufu* troops. Mr. Sawayama did brave service in defending the frontier of his province from the hostile incursion of the enemy.

At the close of the civil war he again gave himself to study, and attended the

---

[1] *Bakufu* was the technical name of the government of the Shogun or Dictator. The family of the Shogun had usurped the temporal power of the Mikado or Emperor, and had ruled with its capital at Yedo for over two hundred and fifty years. In 1868 a revolutionary war opened. The effect of this was to strip the Shogun of his power and restore to the Mikado his authority. The capital was fixed at Yedo, the name of which was changed to Tokyo.

most famous schools of Japan. He not only studied theories, but his whole tendency was to make his knowledge practical.

When he was a boy he listened to a lecture on the sennin. And he was so impressed that he aspired to become a sennin.[1] When Mr. Sawayama returned home from the school he told his parents that he wanted to visit a friend and went away. Instead, however, he ascended a mountain and stayed there several days hoping to become a sennin. When he got hungry he subsisted upon wild fruits or roots of plants, and sometimes he went down to the country and begged food from farmers, and then returned to the mountain again. But he was unsuccessful in these attempts, of course; so he lost all hope of becoming a sennin and returned home. This incident shows his intense

[1] Sennin was the name given to an imaginary being, supposed to be more than a mere man. It denoted a being something like an angel who had been transformed from a man by extraordinary physical and mental exercises.

nature and his determination to realize his ideals.

At one time he heard about a certain Master Shuyo Foshimura, of Shikoku, who was famous not only for his knowledge of the teachings of Confucius, but also for the consistency of his life as a Confucianist. Mr. Sawayama went to him to become his disciple, and in time mastered the ethics and philosophy of the great sage of China.

Civil commotions again threatened to arise, and Mr. Sawayama was put at the head of a band of soldiers and entrusted with the responsibility of suppressing riots. When peace was again restored, his old enthusiasm for study as quickly returned, and he formed a plan for studying Western civilization. With this in view he went to Kobé, where he studied English with Rev. D. C. Greene, D.D., the first Japanese missionary of the American Board. In 1872 he came to America.

Concerning his student life in America,
Mrs. M. C. Wise, who was his instructor at
Evanston, says in The Pacific Advocate:

There is a tradition among Sawayama's countrymen that anyone in the interior desiring
more light or knowledge must go for it to the
coast. Of course the sea coast inhabitants do
possess greater advantages for obtaining infor-
mation. This was especially the case at that
time, when missionaries were not admitted to
the interior.

Sawayama found his way to the coast, a
pilgrim in search of knowledge; and though he
knew it not — in search of God. Reaching the
coast he told his errand, and was pointed to a
little house on the hill. Here he found a missionary (Dr. D. C. Greene). The good man
took Sawayama into his family and told him the
story of the cross. Then it was that he was
converted. Though he did not make a profession
till sometime later, yet after he came to America
and his mind became more and more enlight-
ened and he learned more of spiritual things
he seemed conscious that the work was wrought
for him in Japan.

Sawayama had not resided long in his new
home ere the missionary discovered him to be a

young man of extraordinary qualities of mind
and heart. The good man wrote to friends in
America and secured, in the family of his own
brother, a home for the youth. All was directed by a divine hand, and his home was in
Evanston, Ill., the seat of the Northwestern
University and Garrett Biblical Institute.
Where could there be a more fitting home for
such a mind and heart?

He came to America in 1872. It was that
fall that I first met him. It was a pleasure
to meet the manly, bright-faced, fine-looking
youth as he passed to and fro from the schoolroom, and respond to his low bow and courteous
salutations.

Sawayama's teachers were full of enthusiasm. No scholar in the school was so quiet and
orderly; there was none who learned more
rapidly. Two years later I had the honor to
be for a time his instructor. I can see him now
as he used to stand at the board during mathematics. There were earnest pupils, but no face
wore so earnest a look as his. I remember the
look of perplexity that used to cross his face if
someone was found inattentive or unprepared.
I think he never understood how an eternity-
bound soul could so waste the precious moments
of its probation here.

Sawayama was nearly always the first to turn
from the board with beaming face and upraised
hand to announce the completion of his work.
His tongue, so lately accustomed to our speech,
was all too slow for his rapid thoughts.

Meanwhile his Christian character had
been developing rapidly; but he had as
yet no conviction that it was his duty
to become a preacher. Nor did this conviction come to him for some considerable time. His enthusiasm for Japan
took as yet the more general form of
patriotism.

Mr. L. H. Boutell wrote about Mr.
Sawayama to this writer as follows:—

CHICAGO, June 1, 1892.

MR. J. NARUSE: —

Dear Sir,— The last three years of his resi-
dence here he spent in my family. During his
first three years in this country, he devoted himself to general studies, with the expectation I
think, of entering governmental service on his
return to Japan. About a year before he left
us, one of the Japanese missionaries, Mr. H. H.
Leavitt, visited us and urged him to prepare

himself for missionary work in Japan. He especially impressed upon him the need for Christian labors in Japan at that time.

The result of this conversation was that Mr. Sawayama decided to devote himself to Bible study for a year and then to become a preacher of Christianity to his countrymen. His Bible studies were pursued under the direction of Rev. E. N. Packard, D.D.[1] It was at this time that he took the name Paul, and in his thorough consecration to his work he proved himself not unworthy of the name.

When he decided to devote his life to preaching the gospel among his countrymen, his spirit seemed elevated and quickened by the nobility of his work. He had a consuming zeal for his Master's service. In his consecration to that service, his heroic self-sacrifice, his sensitive conscientiousness, and the childlike simplicity of his faith, he seemed to have caught the spirit of the apostolic age.

What most impressed me, on my first acquaintance with him, was the exquisite refinement of his manners. It was not a mere surface politeness, but sprang from a desire to be of service to others. I do not wonder that he had such an influence among his countrymen,

[1] Now of Syracuse, N. Y.

for here, among ourselves, he won the love of all.   I am, yours truly,

L. H. BOUTELL.

The writer heard from Mr. Sawayama the following account of this experience:

One day, I suppose a little after the interview with Mr. Leavitt, he had been reading the biography of some Christian missionary, and the thought seemed to come to him almost as a revelation, that the need of Japan was the preaching of the Gospel. He thought much, and more and more the conviction grew and strengthened within him that the darkness which covered Japanese society with so many sorrows and sins in its shadow, could never be effectually dissipated except by the power of Christianity; and who could be called of God to preach to Japan, if not himself? He said to his awakened heart: " The people of foreign countries have sacrificed their lives to be missionaries to Japan, how can I see the condition of my own people so indifferently?"

He decided to proclaim upon the house-tops what he had heard in the ear.

The following letter from Rev. E. N. Packard, D.D., to the writer, tells more about Mr. Sawayama's study and other Christian characteristics: —

SYRACUSE, N. Y., July 9, 1892.

MR. J. NARUSE: —

Dear Brother, — Sawayama first appeared in the family of Mr. L. H. Boutell, in Evanston, where I was pastor of the First Congregational Church, and came to church with them and entered the Sunday-school more to learn our language than to become a disciple. But soon he became interested for himself, and in due time declared his faith in Christ. It was with great joy that I received him into the church and administered baptism to him, my first experience in baptizing a foreign-born man.[1]

After this he began to take part in our prayer meetings, now and then. He spoke, of course,

[1] Mrs. M. C. Wise says: "When Sawayama left Japan, his father was required to give bonds to the effect that Sawayama should not change his religion. When he came to make a public profession here he was asked if he did not fear his father would suffer on account of the bonds he had given. Sawayama replied: 'The Lord will take care of that.' And his faith was honored."

very imperfect English, but his words had a peculiar power about them, as if sent by the Spirit. I remember how one of our young men said that that foreign-born and poorly educated young man put to shame those who had been having every advantage.

After a while he began to think of the ministry to his own countrymen, and talked with me about it. He was then in the preparatory department of the Northwestern University, and had several years of work laid out. But something seemed to impress him with the idea that the time was short. Against the judgment of Mr. Boutell and others of us he decided to press for a preparation for the ministry at once, and I arranged with him to come to my study from time to time and to talk over the Christian scheme. We used as a textbook Hodge's Way of Life, and it proved to be an excellent book for the purpose. He became attracted to Paul and his theology, and took the name of Paul for this reason. After weeks of study and conference he suddenly seemed to come out into light and to receive what I can only think of as a "baptism of the Holy Spirit."

His idea as to truth clarified suddenly, and he told me that he felt confident that he could go and meet the objections which his friends in

Japan might bring up. Soon after this, to our surprise, he began to plan to get back to his native land, and his persistence and faith were remarkable. I used to say that, if no other way would offer, Sawayama would take an open boat and row across the Pacific Ocean.

After obtaining help from the Japanese Consul, at New York, and passes from Colonel Hammond, for a part at least of the railroad journey to San Francisco, he bade us farewell and we never saw him again. Mr. Sawayama returned to Japan in 1876. No man ever went to a great task with greater enthusiasm.

I always felt a strong attraction to him, for his many fine qualities and for something indescribable which was the indwelling of the Spirit in him. He had clear views of truth which seemed to have come direct from the source of all truth, direct to him, and not through books. His good nature, his plain and simple scheme of living for Christ were a life-long lesson and blessing to me.   Truly yours,

EDWARD N. PACKARD.

Mrs. Wise says of this period : —

After he yielded to the conviction that it was his duty to go back and labor for the conversion of his people, he seemed to be in a hurry. His

pastor asked him if it would not be better to
remain in Evanston a while longer, where he
would have such fine opportunities for the
study of theology, as well as other branches of
learning, and be more thoroughly prepared for
his work. His reply was: "I have as much
learning as the apostles had." He felt that he
must go quickly, for infidelity was gaining
ground in his country; and he went back to lift
up the standard of the cross.

CHAPTER III.

AT the time of Sawayama's return the majority of the Japanese people hated Christianity "with perfect hatred." They called it "the way of the devils." Native Christians were subjected to various modes and degrees of persecution. Some lost their positions; some were disinherited; many practically were deprived of those social privileges which make freedom valuable. It was a disgrace for a family to have a Christian in its circle. The educated believed in no religion; they despised the native priests and hated the Christian ministers.

Of the few Japanese who then came to America, too many young men who had been converted while students in this country, lost their Christianity in the ocean as they returned to Japan. This

44

is a lamentable fact, but one which will
not be too severely condemned by one
who knows what a Japanese Christian
was called upon to endure in those days.
But Mr. Sawayama came back to his
home with his resolute, devotional, zealous
Christian spirit undaunted. But in another respect he found that Christianity
had made great progress in Japan. He
says in his letter as follows : —

OSAKA, Japan, October 17, 1876.
REV. EDWARD PACKARD : —

Dear Friend, — When I reached Yokohama
I found all the features of the city and people
so much changed from what I used to see five
years ago. Many streets and buildings are constructed in the European style, and the government buildings are, of course, constructed in
fine European styles in all plans. Systems of
post office and others are well adapted to that of
Americans, and I think that we are almost as con-
venient in most cases in Japan as in America.
I am much surprised to see that the education of
Japan is very much progressed. I think that
the degree of studies in our colleges and high

schools is as high as common American colleges
and high schools. Once I visited with Mr.
Nakahara, while I was staying in Tokyo, a
girls' high school, and it was the examination
day. I heard a few classes. They were in
natural philosophy, arithmetic, geometry, etc.,
and I noticed that they all recited quite well.
On the way to my home from Yokohama, I was
very much pleased to see the flags on the poles,
which are signs of public schools. They were
seen here and there in every town and village.
The schools in Japan are indeed in flourishing
condition. I was much ashamed to have found,
when I reached my home, that my brother
knows geography and arithmetic better than I
do.

Above all things, I was very much rejoiced to
have found the advancement of Christian religion in Japan. Though I had heard a good
deal about the success of the missions when I
was in America, as you know, I was hardly
prepared to find their work so fully arranged.
I met most of the brethren in Yokohama, and
I was requested to preach at Otamachi Chapel,
and so I did. This chapel is situated in the midst
of one of the busiest streets in this city; the
people crowd to hear the gospel quietly. I
attended several Christian meetings in this city,

and I believe that all the brethren are earnest and enthusiastic workers for Christ, and I enjoyed the meeting every time. I found, when I went to Tokyo, one of my old friends had become a faithful Christian.

I stayed but one week with Mr. Greene, in Yokohama. During the time, I had a very joyful time indeed, and then I sailed to Kobé from Yokohama. In Kobé I did not stay many days, though I preached once in the chapel, one Sunday, and in the evening I was invited to take tea with Miss Talcot, in the girl's seminary, and had great pleasure in meeting with the many enthusiastic girls as I thought. It happened that I was in at the time of their evening prayer-meeting. There were but about a dozen girls, as most of the students were gone home for the vacation, as I was told. They prayed for nearly all interests of the world, and half dozen or more girls continued to pray in one kneeling.

In Osaka, I stayed with my old friend Mr. Utsumi, the vice-governor of the city, and I could not see any of our missionary friends here, as they were then all gone away from the city, for the summer vacation.

From Osaka, straightway I went to my home and I found my mother, sister, and brother were quite well. My sister and brother were grown up so very big that I thought I should not know them if I had met them anywhere else than at home; but my father looked very bad as he has been very sick. They were greatly rejoiced at my return home, after a very long absence. My father said: "My son, now you come home, so my sickness will be better by and by I think." When I told them the great kindness which I received in America my parents expressed uttermost gratefulness, and wished me to thank for them, my American friends, through my pen. My father said he would go to thank you, the Evanston friends, for the kindness, if America were not such a distant land. My friends at home heard me to speak of Christ, with much interest. Although I did not see an actual success in the work at home, yet I hope that some good will be done for their unbelieving hearts by the talk and by the religious books which I left them.

After about ten days' stay at home, I came back to this city; although my parents wished me to stay at home all the time and not go away from them any more, yet I felt that I better come here to work. As my father is quite sick, I am anxious about him very much, while I stay here, and I hope that I may visit home as often as I can, but it is difficult to go home often, for many reasons.

Please give my Christian love to your family and to all my friends in Evanston, both young and old. Tell that I am thinking about them all the time, and hope to be friends with them continually in this life and the next too. Hoping you will always be successful in your works, and may God bless you,

Yours affectionately,

P. U. SAWAYAMA.

His parents were quite disappointed that Mr. Sawayama was converted to Christianity, though they were very glad of his safe return home. But Mr. Sawayama merely waited, and with great patience, for the conversion of his parents. He had a profound filial love for them, and wherever it did not involve a compromise of his Christian principles he accommodated his life to their wishes.

As an instance of this disposition towards his parents I will mention a little incident which occurred during a sickness of his father : —

Mr. Sawayama had become accustomed while in America to the cold sponge baths which are so invigorating to begin the day with, and he disliked exceedingly to dip his weak body, for he was by no means strong, into the hot water of the Japanese baths. This contempt, for so he deemed it, of Japanese customs, displeased his father greatly, and he in return refused to take some medicine which Mr. Sawayama was sure would be very beneficial to him.

"You refuse to take a hot bath and I will not take your medicine," said he.

Mr. Sawayama answered immediately, " Father, take the medicine, please; I will take the hot bath."

In many such ways he sought to serve his parents, though it might be at the expense of his own comfort.

But he could not stay longer at home. He removed to Osaka city to begin his work there. No matter how busy he might be — and he was very busy — and no matter how completely his attention

and sympathies were engrossed in the
work of his ministry, he never neglected
to write to his parents, to send them good
books and to pray for them. It was not
long before his whole family was converted to Christianity.

As Mr. Sawayama's clan had ardently
championed the cause of the Mikado it
had come out of the revolution with great
éclat. Many of his friends had important
and honorable positions in the new government which had lately been established.
A new civilization was dawning in Japan.
The government, quick to appreciate the
needs and the opportunities of the hour,
sought to secure the ablest men for their
service. Those who had studied in civil-
ized countries and might thus be supposed
to have the spirit of Western civilization
were in especial requisition. Every in-
ducement was offered in the way of
salaries.

Those friends of Mr. Sawayama who
held government positions brought their

influence to bear upon him to induce him
to accept one.   They knew his ability, but
they did not know his Christian constancy.
"Counting the reproach of Christ greater
riches than the treasures" of this world,
he chose "rather to be evil-entreated with
the people of God."   Finding a little
band of eleven despised Christians he
promised to be their pastor.

The self-sacrifice of this act becomes
more apparent when it is remembered that
such a governmental position as was offered to Mr. Sawayama would have paid
him from the beginning one hundred and
fifty dollars [1] a month, while his little con-
gregation could pay him but seven dollars.
It became still more apparent when it
is added that Mr. Sawayama was in debt
to his father and his friends for a considerable part of his education, and was
in such physical condition as to require
for his comfort many things which he

---

[1] Equivalent in purchasing power to $8,000 or $9,000 per
year in the United States.

could not at such a meager salary ever
hope to have. But he said to himself
"If any man will seek first the kingdom
of God and his righteousness," all these
things will be added unto him, and he
received with simplicity and sincerest
gratitude the seven dollars of his salary.
The abundance which the government
might have given him he cared not for.
His fellow-Christians out of their poverty
had freely given unto him, and he was
very happy.

From the beginning Mr. Sawayama
held very firmly to the principle that
Japanese Christianity should be self-supporting. His aim was to found a living
Japanese church; to put within it such a
spirit of growth and independence as
should set it free from its slavish, feeble
condition; to make it a permanent power
by the force of its own religious life.
This he thought should be the aim of
every Japanese Christian.

I suppose this principle of self-support

Mr. Sawayama received from Rev. H. H. Leavitt at Evanston when they conversed with each other; and it had grown up to be his ideal scheme of mission work in Japan.

What did Mr. Sawayama mean by self-support for Japanese churches? This question will be answered in his own words later, in the speech he delivered at the great conference; but here I may say that he meant that the Japanese churches should pay their own expenses, meeting all the expenditures required for home missionary work, for Christian education, and for church benevolences, without receiving pecuniary aid for these purposes from foreign missionary societies. Those societies of course should continue to support their own missionaries. This program proved a very difficult task for such poor bodies as the Japanese churches: so almost all of the native Christians, except his church, and many foreign missionaries, could not approve of his new scheme at that time.

But Mr. Sawayama had a rare insight into the condition of the time and future of Japan. There were a few Japanese Christian churches and Christian schools at that early day, but they had been started by means of foreign funds and were managed by the missionaries. The vast majority of the Japanese people were intensely prejudiced against them because they seemed to be in reality foreign churches and foreign schools. They also thought that the foreigners propagated their religion by the lavish use of money. Quite often the native Christians were asked if they received money from foreigners in order to become Christians. Sometimes these haters of Christianity called the Christians beggars because they depended upon foreign funds, and accused them of disloyalty to their own country. It must be confessed that the native Christians showed a strong tendency to rely upon the financial aid of foreigners in every department of Christian work.

They seemed to entertain the feeling that they were the guests of the universal Christian Church, and as such were entitled to free entertainment, as Mr. Sawayama said in his famous speech. In such circumstances there was great need of insistence upon the principle of self-support. And there is no question that Mr. Sawayama's persistence in advocating that principle gave to the Japanese church its strength and aggressiveness.

In 1877 Mr. Sawayama was ordained by Mr. Neesima and a company of missionaries, over the Naniwa Church in Osaka, which had eleven members. Mr. Sawayama was thus the first man to be established as pastor over a Japanese church.

Just before his ordination he wrote Mrs. Boutell, about his work in Osaka, as follows : —

OSAKA, Japan, January 8, 1877.

Dear Mrs. Boutell, — The climate in this city is milder than most of the places in Japan in the same latitude. We have had only very little snow for several days, this winter. My health is improving all the time, though I have more or less cough day and night.

As I wrote you last time, I have still my Sunday-school, and preaching service at Dr. Adams' dispensary, which is situated on the corner of two flourishing streets in the city. Both audiences and power are increasing in our services in this place with wonderful success. I have no doubt that God helps us with great power to convert the people of this great city.

Some gentlemen from Sanda (the place of which you heard so much), who live in the drug store just in front of the dispensary building, told me the other day that they have heard much about " this way " in Kobé and Sanda; but they did not study deeply about this way although they did not think badly of it. Since they came to live in the drug store, they could come regularly to hear our preaching and study the Bible in our Sunday-school, and so the truths of Christianity impressed deeply their hearts. One of them said to me with repented expression in his face, that he believes now there is one Almighty God in the universe and he is a great sinner toward him, which he did not believe before, and he is going to receive baptism and join the Kobé church as soon as he shall go back to Kobé. Now they are diligently studying the Bible with me in the Sunday-school, and in my room.

One of the higher officers of the Osaka government, who is my very old friend, is diligently studying the Bible with me on Sunday and on evenings, and I think that he will become a Christian by and by, though he told me the other day that he would not be baptized at present, because he is an officer, but he would study the Bible all the time, and help Christianity as much as he could in his power. But I hope that he won't say very soon "I will not be baptized because I am an officer."

The vice-governor of the city, who is also my most intimate friend, is an intelligent and kind-hearted man. Though he does not care to know about Christianity, he does not make any trouble for us, I think. When I asked him if he would not study the Bible with me, he answered me that he has so much to do all the time and has no time for such a study. As I go to his house most every day, I talked about this way to his wife and she gladly hears the truth. She has bought "Peep of the Day," and is interested in it very much. I made the Christmas present to the vice-governor and his wife with "Evidences of Christianity" and "Gospel" and other religious books, and they thanked me very much. Their son and servants come to hear me to preach sometimes.

It seems to me that God's own good time has come to impress powerfully the gospel truth into men's hearts here in this city. Christian light is in the state of the rising sun, and shining brighter and brighter in the dark land.

Last month I asked the vice-governor, who had just returned from Tōkyō, what is the most flourishing thing in Tōkyō. He answered me that the most flourishing thing is Christianity and most declining thing is drinking. I thought this answer was not untruth, and we must rejoice for it and work for Christ more earnestly.

Yesterday was the communion Sunday and Osaka church received thirteen members by confession of faith and one by letter and baptized two children of believing parents. About five more persons are waiting to be baptized to join the new church which will be formed within a few weeks I think, and of which I will be the pastor if God will.

There are now a great many other preaching places in this city. Dr. Yamamoto, who is one of our most distinguished physicians, has invited us to preach in his private hospital. One preaching place is in Shinmachi Street which was a most noted prostitution den; another in Houden and many other places. . . .

Give my love to all your household and all my friends both in Evanston and in Chicago. (They are so many that I cannot mention their names separateiy.)

Most affectionately yours,
PAUL SAWAYAMA.

Mr. Sawayama wrote again after his ordination to Mrs. Boutell : —

Osaka, Japan, February 23, 1877.

We joyfully formed a new church of Christ which is called " Naniwa Church of Christ," and I was ordained as pastor of the church. It was the twentieth of last month. The services of the day were very grand and successful. I wish that you could have been with us on that day.

I have in my church only eleven members, of which eight are men and three are women, but they are all active preachers, and we have at present five regular preaching places for the church beside our own chapel, and so we are quite busy, but it is a very joyful thing to be busy in the Master's work. I never have experienced so much joy in my heart as these

days. I tell you, Mrs. Boutell and my Christian
friends in Evanston, that it is a joyful thing to
work hard for Christ, as you clearly know. I
write you the following about our church service during the week: —

Sunday. 10 A.M. to 11, Preaching.

11 to 12, Bible Study.

3 P.M. to 4.30 Sunday-school.

7 P.M., Preaching.

Monday. 7 P.M., Bible Study.

Wednesday. 7 P.M., Prayer-meeting.

Thursday. 7 P.M., Bible Study.

Friday. 7 P.M., General Prayer-meeting.

Pray for me, my dear friends, that I may
have great faith and wisdom in Christ, that I
may be fit to work for Christ as pastor of the
flock; and pray for the little church. I pray
for you all.　　　Affectionately yours,

PAUL SAWAYAMA.

This Naniwa Church was like a grain
of mustard seed in its beginning. But it
grew very rapidly; at the end of five
years it had increased its yearly contribution from seventy dollars to seven hundred dollars. It had started an inde
pendent church in Osaka city, and made

a beginning of Christian work in nine other places. It had established a Christian girls' school in the city. That the church had had such rapid growth, starting as it did in the midst of so many prejudices and difficulties, so great poverty and suspicion, must be attributed largely to Mr. Sawayama's great faith and Christian character.

The following letter shows us his work during those days : —

I suppose that my church was organized in January, 1877, with eleven members. Since that time by the missionary efforts two churches have been formed, both of whose pastors are members of my church. Last year we received fifty persons by profession and three by letter. Total contributions for the last year were seven hundred and twenty-six yen, the yen being now of the value of about a dollar.

My church raised this money from the poorest people, who own neither house nor anything, hardly.

We must recognize that the Japanese wages and prices are both very low.

Therefore the seven hundred and twenty-six dollars was a quite good sum for such a church in Japan.[1]

Mr. Sawayama was careful to establish a good foundation for the church; so he helped the young converts to root out their sins and start a vigorous new Christian life.

To the friends at Evanston he wrote:—

OSAKA, Japan, May 18, 1877.

I thank you for sending me the certificate of my church membership, and I was very glad to hear from Rev. Edward Packard so kind and sympathetic a message. May we always be connected by the strong chain of love of Jesus Christ our Lord and our Saviour! I was very glad to hear from Mrs. Boutell such thorough and minute news of our Evanston friends. When I was reading her letter I felt almost as if I were to see them by face to face.

My church work is going on quite nicely. Our church members are united together in the same

---

[1] The purchasing value of one yen or Japanese dollar would be expressed in the United States by about $5, though the actual exchange value of the yen is simply that of the trade dollar. Seven hundred and twenty-six yen would thus purchase as much in Japan as $3,500 would in America.

mind and in the same judgment in love and faithfulness to our Redeemer. God blessed our work and we received several applications to join our church; but we do not hasten to receive them, as we must examine them thoroughly, so that we may (as far as our human mind can judge, although we cannot say that we proved the depth of the heart) prove that they are true Christians and are willing to sacrifice all things for Christ's sake, even their own lives if it is necessary.

Some of the applicants were most bigoted Buddhists. They are working now among their former religious friends; I hope they will lead many of those who are in the darkness into the light of the Christian religion. One of the applicants is a doctor; he is faithful and fervent in spirit: he preaches to every sick man as he goes round for his practice. One of the regular attendants to the church is a barber; he shuts his shop on Sunday and comes to church regularly; he keeps religious tracts and newspapers in his shop and preaches to people while he is cutting their hair or shaving them. One of the merchants is interested in the way and attends the church every Sabbath and also he opens his house for religious services. His four servants are very much interested in this way, and one of them is ready to unite with the church, but he is waiting to join with the other three. Their neighbors noticed that their conduct had changed, and that they had become so very honest and kind since they had become Christians (though they do not yet receive baptism), and these neighbors also have begun to come to church. Don't you think Christians are truly the light of the world? Eighty-two of Kobé prisoners are converted, as I heard from Mayeda San, who is chief officer in the prison; he is a Christian, of course. I went to see them the other day; they are quite hopeful ones.

Our church members are all active preachers, men as well as women, and have their own places to preach regularly. I have preaching or instructing services every day, except Saturday, on which I prepare for Sunday services. I am quite busy in my works, but they are not heavy to carry on. Christ's burden is light and his yoke is easy.

My parents wrote me the other day that the neighbors speak evil of them because they are interested in Christianity; so they asked me to pray to the true God to protect them and bless them, and I wrote them in answer that persecution for Christ's sake is sign of favor of God, and comforted them, and told them to read the eleventh and twelfth verses of the fifth chapter of Matthew.

All my church members send you much Christian love. I have told them many times about you and the Evanston Church. They think a great deal of you.

Dr. Gordon, whom we love greatly, is obliged to go to his home in America on account of his eyes. We are very sorry to part with him. May God bless him and restore him in good health again before very long and let him come back again to work among us!

I send you articles for presents to you. These are small tokens of my great love. You will please find the list of presents in this paper and distribute them according to the list.

Your sincerest friend and brother in Christ,
PAUL SAWAYAMA.

To Mrs. Boutell : —

Your two letters and one of Mr. Boutell's have been received. I did not get them as soon as I ought, on account of my occasional absence from Osaka, during the summer, for my sister's death and others. I am exceedingly glad to know that you are all well and prosperous by the merciful providence of our heavenly Father.

I spent a little while with Mr. and Mrs.

Greene this summer in Arima and I enjoyed it more than anything else this summer. I have a great affection toward their children, and the children also like me very much, I think. Whenever we meet together they want me to play with them, which makes me quite tired. When they went to bed they all came to kiss me. The day I was leaving them in Arima, Jerome said to his mother: "Mamma, I want to eat up Sawayama San before he leaves us." Then Mrs. Greene said: "O Jerome, some one in the Kobé School will feel very badly if you should eat Sawayama San up."

"Some one in Kobé School" meant my intended wife, who is teaching Chinesed Japanese in Kobé School, of whom you may have heard already either from Mr. Greene or from Mrs. Greene.

Our annual meetings in Kobé were very interesting. At the meeting I was kindly asked by Mr. and Mrs. Greene to baptize their dear baby, Mary Avery Greene, and I thankfully performed the service.

One who received baptism lately in my church was a doctor who is about sixty years old. He was a most bigoted Buddhist. When we examined him it was satisfactory in every matter, and then we asked him if he would give up anything which does not honor Christ and does not make him a useful man, even if the thing may not be bad or wicked, and he said he would. Then we asked him to give up his smoking, which is not for any honor for Christ, though we do not say that those who smoke are not true Christians. He said that he was willing to give up. Few days after he sent word that we should wait his baptism till next time on account of that he cannot yet give up his smoking. Then I went to see him and I noticed that he was reading Bible and praying and fasting. He told me that he has been smoking day and night during these forty years, therefore it is very hard for him to give it up. But he said that he is willing to give up even his life for Christ's sake, if it need be. Why cannot smoking be given up? Because he thinks his faith is not yet strong, so he will pray God to give strong faith to overcome these habits; and that time we kneeled and prayed together, and few days after that he succeeded to give it up entirely.

This doctor led an old couple who were also strong Buddhists. Since they gave up associating with their former friends the former friends with priests came to their house many times to try to lead them back to the former

faith, but they told them that this is the true
way, so they had better come to hear about the
way. They brought the priest to our church
and they are now trying to lead Buddhists to
hear the gospel of Christ. Our elder, Mayegami San, goes to his house to preach every
Friday. This old couple's story is very long
and interesting, but I have not time to write all
this morning.

When I went home this summer I found
one young man who had become very much
interested in Christianity. He came to study
Bible every day while I was there and when I
came back to Osaka he also came with me as
far as to Kobé. In that place he has a cousin
who is a higher officer. This young man decided to be a minister, but his cousin tried to
persuade him to become an officer. But if he
should become an officer, he cannot sometimes
keep the Sabbath. So he told his cousin that he
preferred rather to be a slave to keep God's
holy law than to become an officer to break it;
so he was obliged to depart from him immediately. He came here last Saturday and is waiting for baptism. His faith is increasing greatly.

I received a letter with "Christian Voice"
from Robert McLean. I thank him for them
very much and I meant to write him by this

mail, but I am afraid that I could not do so by this; but I will answer him anyway before long. If you should see him, please tell him about it.

I have not at all written to any friends both in Evanston and Chicago, besides your own family, for I have not such sufficient knowledge in English as to write English letter rapidly; therefore writing English makes me quite awkward. Perhaps that makes some friends to feel that I do not remember them; but yes, yes! I do remember them all the time and think about them and pray for them in public and in closet. In my pocketbook many addresses of my American friends are written, for I meant to write them; but since I came back to my country I never could yet accomplish what I want in this. Will you tell them our friends there and elsewhere the above condition wherever you should meet together?

Most affectionately yours,
PAUL SAWAYAMA.

To Mrs. Boutell: —

Though I am not yet attending the evening meeting of the church, Deacon Mayegami is taking charge of them, and the works of my church are going on very nicely now. It seems it has pleased God to prosper the work of our churches here. The last month, Temma Church (which is a daughter of my church) received several students of the Osaka College. I baptized one on the first Sunday.

I commenced my work last month and have now several persons who wish to come into my church, so we are now examining them in order to receive them by the next communion service. The First Church is also going to receive about five persons at the same time.

Many students of the college above are attending regularly the meetings of our churches through the influence chiefly of their teachers, Tamura and Koidsumi, who are members of the church. Over half a dozen of them were already received into the churches. The president of the college, Mr. Hattori, formerly the vice-president of the Imperial University, is my childhood friend and schoolmate, and is very kind to me, though he is in religion a disciple of Darwin. He is the graduate of the same college in which Dr. D. C. Greene graduated. He invited me a few weeks ago to the college and showed me the medical, chemical, and other college departments. They are all taught by the Japanese professors.

P. SAWAYAMA.

To Rev. Edward Packard: —

OSAKA, Japan, March 26, 1880.

I hope, if it be the will of the Lord, that I should be spared longer to serve him in the work in which he has blessed me very much these several years since I came back from America.[1] I have been exceedingly happy in the work which the Lord directed my heart to decide as my life service to him. Indeed this joy which I received from him, the world in any circumstances could not take away from me.

My dear pastor, I never even one day could forget you, and my American friends, as you were the means of my conversion. I began to take charge of the daily religious exercises of our girls' school a few weeks ago as I used to do before. You know we started this school two years ago by our own hand with the good advices of the missionaries, and we built the schoolhouse last year. Now we have over fifty scholars who are all very nice girls and most of them are from the families of high class. I am very glad that I could have the opportunity to tell much about the Saviour to them and help

---

[1] Mr. Sawayama already had consumption at this time.

them to come to him. Several of them are already members of my church.

Yours sincerely,

PAUL SAWAYAMA.

Mr. Sawayama had a peculiar magnetic power. No one made him a visit or talked with him without receiving a good impression from him. Every Christian who came to him for help or advice was certain to receive all that he expected. I will refer to the two following instances out of many : —

Mr. Tomoyoshi Murai, who is now a student in Andover Seminary, told me the other day his impression of Mr. Sawayama : —

"Ever since I had heard of Mr. Sawayama as a man of faith and character, I had expected for a long time to see him ; finally I had a short interview with him while he was in the hospital. I have never forgotten the pure and celestial influences that I received from him. I was greatly helped and inspired by his talks.

I recall that I was then anxious to convert my father, who had heard of Christianity for six years, who sought to become a Christian himself but could not do so on account of his doubts and perplexities, and yet was highly interested in Christianity and induced his wife and daughters to join the church, and gave all possible help to the extension of Christianity in his town.

"I presented the case before Mr. Sawayama and asked him how to lead such a one to Christ. He advised me not to be overanxious about it, but to wait trustfully for God's time. God may convert him in some unexpected way. He told me then the story of Whitefield's conversion and of others who were brought to Christ not through any efforts of their fellow men, but through a combination of certain circumstances. Whitefield, he said, was stopping in the hotel when he recalled that Christ was born in a hotel, and then his conversion took place.

" Wonderful it was that after a few years my father made his decision to become a Christian in a similar manner as Mr. Sawayama suggested. One Sunday he was left at home alone while all the rest went to church. He heard the church bell ringing, which sounded to his ears like God's call to his soul, which proved to be a turning point in his life and made him enter the kingdom of God."

The other case is told of by Mr. Sawayama himself in one of his letters as follows : —

One night a woman came to me burdened with her sins, and I tried to show her what seemed to be her duty. After praying with her she went home, and before retiring she tried to give up all to Christ and accept his salvation. In the morning her heart was full of joy, and as she had no desire for the bad habit to which she been tempted as usual, she took that as one of the signs that her heart was changed. As her health was very poor her family urged her to go to her native country for a change; but soon after reaching there she received a letter of divorce from her husband. She was thus thrown upon her family for support, and she must be dependent upon her brother, as her parents were not living.

On returning to her brother's house she did not, as formerly, worship the household gods, and her brother was very angry. He said to her: "If you will not worship and offer food and flowers to the gods, you cannot stay in my house: you are a disgrace to the family, even neglecting the ancestral tablets." Her sister-in-law, although not so angry, urged her to give up her God, and worship as they did, while she lived in their house.

She replied: "I cannot give up my God. Even though my brother should whip me to death I cannot give him up."

Finally her brother opened the bureau drawers and taking out her clothing and everything that belonged to her, threw them out in the yard, telling her to leave his house.

The woman was in sore trouble, as she in her poor health was being driven away from the only house she had. But she had been praying for guidance and soon her way was made plain. A man came telling her that he was in search of a woman to teach needlework to a class of girls in an adjoining town and had heard of her.

Would she be willing to go? She was of course glad to go. She stayed there a few months, when her husband, having become a Christian, went and brought her back to her Osaka home.

They seem very happy and are together trying to work in bringing others to the services and in teaching them at home.

Even those who hated Christianity admired his Christian virtues. Mr. Sawayama had no enemy. I remember a great Confucian scholar who said : " Mr. Sawayama is a sage indeed." To the Confucianist the ideal man is the sage, the possessor of true wisdom.

His church was characterized by a spirit of broad sympathy and love. There were no divisions in it. Not only was his church devoted to him, but his personal influence reached out until all the Christians of Japan loved him. And this influence did not depend on his eloquence, but upon the power of his Christian personality. Dr. De Forest, one of the most

prominent missionaries in Japan, says of
Mr. Sawayama, in his letter to Mr. and
Mrs. Boutell : —

We only hope he may be spared to encourage
his church, hoping against hope. There is no
church like his in all Japan; none so noted for
generosity; none that has set so high an example
for active and pure Christian living. Churches
two hundred miles away have learned to speak
of Mr. Sawayama's church as *the* one to pattern
after. So that we have every reason to pray for
his health and strength to be continued to us.
He has already two plans on foot: one to build
a church, the other, to establish a boys' school.
If he is spared to us, it may be that we should
be very glad to avail ourselves of your kind
offer of help.

Another missionary in writing of him
says : —

He is a burning and shining light in this great
city. It is wonderful how near he keeps to his
Saviour though surrounded by heathen influences and customs. His life is as simple as that
of a little child, and I believe as pure. He
seems to trust God perfectly, and when the way
is darkest his faith is strongest.

Soon after his return from America he was attacked by a disease which rapidly developed into consumption. From this time until his death he had scarcely one comfortable day, during a period of ten years. His work was done rather upon his sick bed than in the pulpit, and during five years five coffins were carried out from his home. His younger sister died soon after his return to Japan. After a long illness his father died. Mr. Sawayama received a telegram from his father to come immediately, when he was himself enfeebled and his wife was on a sick bed. He says in a letter: —

Our baby daughter was born on the twelfth of the last October. Her name is Isa. . . . My father died at his home on the twenty-first of last October. He became a believer in Christ, and about ten days before his death telegraphed to me to come to see him, and accordingly I left this city on the third day after my baby's birth, and I was with him and baptized him. His last days were very pleasant and thankful, and he died happy in believing Christ. My thanks cannot be expressed for it. My mother and brother are also Christians now, I think.

Some Americans said of this: "In the interior of Japan a son performing the holy ordinance of baptism for a believing father."

Then his child and his mother died. He writes: —

We had two daughters, but one died last year. Within a few years since I left you, I think I have experienced several conditions of human life: I became pastor, husband, and father; and lost father, sister, child, and mother. I thank God, all these joys and sorrows of my life bring me closer to Christ who is "the same yesterday, and to-day and forever."

And last of all his beloved wife died, leaving him with his little daughter. Though Mr. Sawayama was himself enfeebled and rendered miserable by diseases, he never ceased in his devotion to these sufferers, comforting them in every way and guiding them by his words and his love to their eternal peace. In a letter

he says: "My wife died on the thirtieth
of May, 1884. A year before her death
she experienced a great change in her
spiritual life. In her sickness and death
she was very, very happy."

How came this new experience to Mrs.
Sawayama? A year before her death she
began to doubt of her salvation and feared
to die. She called her husband and cling-
ing to his sleeves cried bitterly on account
of the uncertainty of her salvation. Mr.
Sawayama, while usually full of affection and tender love to her, at that occasion bravely forsook her in the view of
her soul's welfare, saying, " I am your
husband, but I am not your Saviour.
You have been relying on me more than
on Christ. You made a tremendous mistake. I love you, but cannot save your
soul. Christ is your Saviour and he
alone. Call upon him and seek your salvation." Then he left her alone and
came downstairs. She struggled severely
but was finally driven to Christ, forsaking

all her temporal reliances and surrendering herself entirely to Jesus.

In a letter to the writer which he wrote after his wife died, he says: "Unosuke [his younger brother, who went to Doshisha College] and Mrs. Naruse and Isa [his four-year-old daughter who came to my home, where I and my wife took care of her for a long while as Mr. Sawayama was sick], departed from me this morning, so I felt very lonesome."

Again he says to Mrs. Boutell: "I naturally feel a great loss of my wife and am very lonely, but thank God she died very peacefully with firm faith in Christ, and both her sickness and death blessed many. My grateful feeling toward God for her is, 'Thou hast made her most blessed for ever. Thou has made her exceedingly glad with thy countenance.'

"I am now sick in the hospital, so I cannot work much, but I am praying constantly and the work of my church is blessed. Please pray for my work, which is God's."

There is a Japanese poem which Mr. Sawayama wrote in a few minutes to comfort his wife when she was subjected to severe pain through her disease, which is translated as follows : —

Spare thou our lives or take them, Lord,
  Our deepest hearts at peace shall be,
Our earthly frames with glad accord
  To all thy will, we trust to thee.

If, by thy grace, our lives are spared,
  We 'll serve thee through our earthly days,
We 'll linger here, with souls prepared
  To render thee eternal praise.

If thou shouldst call us in our youth,
  We 'll hasten through the open gate
Without regret, for there, in truth,
  Thy many mansions for us wait.

The bitter pains and struggles sore
  Through which our lives are passing now,
Thou knewest them, Saviour, all before:
  Thou leadest us; to thee we bow.

For all who strive to enter in
  Thy heavenly kingdom, Master, God,
Must walk with anguish over sin,
  The thorny path thyself hast trod.

His burdens did not stop here; for he had, like Paul, " the care of the churches." He must continue his own preaching, guide his own work, oversee the management of his school and missions. But he was never disappointed, never uttered one word of displeasure or complaint. He was always courageous, thankful, cheerful, and hopeful.

Once he wrote to the writer as follows : " Your sympathetic letters comforted me very much. My wife is on her sick bed still. I had a hemorrhage of the lungs yesterday, but I feel a little better to-day. . . . My family is in the calamity of disease all the time, but I am rejoicing and thanking day and night, because I have learned the way of rejoicing in every trouble."

And he said again at another time : " My wife and myself are in severe sickness, but the grace of God is increasing according to the proportion of the afflictions."

Many times my own heart was stirred

to deep sorrow on his behalf, but he said, not with the spirit of resignation but rather of a deep thankfulness: " Naked came I out of my mother's womb, and naked shall I return thither; the Lord gave, and the Lord hath taken away; blessed be the name of the Lord." And if I saw the tears gathered in his eyes while we sang the funeral hymns, it was not so much the expression of sorrow as of a profound emotion of thankfulness for the great salvation which had come to him and to his household.

His doctors often wondered greatly at his physical endurance. They appointed many times beyond which he could not live. But his weak body was sustained by the spirit of faith and courage in which he lived. He did not care much about his body, but he aspired all the time to the development of his spirit only. His soul was all; his body was but little. The following letters show us this stage of his disease and his courage.

To Mrs. Boutell, October 30, 1877 : —

My health is not very good. I mean by that
I have had trouble in my head these five months
more or less, and now I feel much worse and I
cannot do much work, as I have nervous headache day and night. Dr. Adams tried me with
medicines; but I do not feel any better; but I
believe that if I should rest for a little while
from my daily work, I should be more well I
hope. As I feel that everything comes from
the Almighty hand of our Merciful Father in
heaven, I feel that I learned a good lesson by
the sickness. He teaches me to depend more
upon his strength which is infinite, instead of
depending on my feeble strength and wisdom.
So I rejoice even in my weakness.

Every one of my church members is trying to
work for our dear Saviour with the utmost
strength. They are willing to sacrifice all, and
I think they all almost try to say boldly with
St. Paul: "For to me to live is Christ and to
die is gain."

In his letter to the same on February
4, 1878, he says : —

I have still headache nearly all the time, and
so I went to Himeji to rest a little while last

November, but I could not get well. I think
I have brain disease, because I have such a long
time since the commencement of my headache.
Also Dr. Adams told me decidedly that I will
not live long because I have consumption. I am
very careful for my health and walk round the
city for exercise most all day, and preach sermons out doors. But I do not feel weak at all.
I could say almost to any one who salute me:
"How do you do?" "I am very well, thank you."
This constant headache, as Dr. Adams thinks,
comes from hectic fever; but thank God I am
very successful in the work which my heavenly
Father gave me to do, and am very happy.

This morning one missionary said to me,
"Good morning, Mr. Sawayama. You are always bright and happy these days." I think it
is better to be happy than well; is it not? I
think that is very true.

He says again in a letter of November,
18, 1878: —

"I have been feeling quite unwell, as the
doctor thought I could not live long. But I am
thankful to God, that in these days of my ill
health, I have never even been discouraged, as
I really know from my heart that I am entirely
in the hand of our heavenly Father who loved

me, and sent his Son to die for me. I thank
God that I am able to say from my heart, "The
Lord's will be done," either in my life or death.

By the blessing of God, I am much improving in my health these days, so I am very glad
that I could work daily for Christ more than
before, and I hope that my health will continually improve, if it is God's will. Indeed I have,
by God's grace, a great ambition to serve the
work which God gave me to do in this world,
forgetting what an unworthy man I am. Yet
I believe by faith that great apostle's words,
"I can do all things through Christ who
strengtheneth me," and I am willing to sacrifice
joyfully for Christ's sake all my comforts, ease,
and honor in the world, if it is necessary, and
try to follow him more closely, who had not
where to lay his head on earth. But beyond my
hope, God blessed me with many comforts and
kind friends, honor and other innumerable
blessings.

To-morrow my wife and I will go to Kishi-
nowadda, a city which is twenty miles south of
this city. I have already been there to preach
twice before. This is the country of ex-
daimio (the prince) who is now in Springfield,
Mass., and was converted there. He wrote the
people to hear the gospel, and so they invited

us to come to preach for them. I have an audience of one hundred and fifty people every time. I promised to go there to preach every other week. I preach at three o'clock in the afternoon and seven in the evening. Now they want me to teach them with book in the hour between the two meetings. Hereafter I will take my wife with me and let her teach the women and also teach singing.

To-night we are going to have our sociable, which we have on every other Monday evening. In these meetings we all get a great deal of benefit in uniting together Christians as brethren and sisters as we talk together everything very familiarly.

I will not write you any more now, as I must attend to some business of the Home Missionary Society, which we established last spring, because we are going to have our annual meeting in Kobé next Friday.

On October 7, 1878, he says:—

I am also not well all the time. I have more or less fever, headache, cough, and so general feebleness in my entire body. Yet I am very thankful that I believe that "all things work together for good to them that love God, to them who are the called, according to his

purpose," and am able to say, in whatever condition I may be, "All well, Lord!"

At one time before the death of his
wife, he suffered from the fiercest attack
of his disease. At the same time his
wife was sick with a severe hemorrhage
of the lungs and a very high fever. Mr.
Sawayama could not sleep, or even lie
down for seven days and nights, so
severe was his pain; during all this time
he remained almost motionless upon the
floor, in a position which I can scarcely
describe so as to make the reader see it.
But as nearly as I can describe it it was
this: he kneeled, bringing his hips close
down to his ankles, then threw his body
forward upon the floor, resting it upon
his elbows, which were drawn back under
his chest, and supporting his head with
his hands. I was taking care of him and
his sick wife as best I could. I often
offered to rub his muscles so as to relieve
him somewhat, but he would not allow
me to remit my care of his wife for so

long a time. Remaining in this position
he did not speak for seven days, but
waited calmly and patiently. As soon
as his distress began to lessen a little he
smiled and said to me: "I never prayed
that the Father would take my soul, for
it would be a selfish prayer. I am glad to
stay in this world and to endure my pain
as long as the Father wishes." Then he
added: "If at any time death comes, it
shall make no difference to me. I will
do just the same work just before my
death as at any other time." He said
often: "I will die on the battlefield; I
will fight the good fight." And not even
his great namesake said more bravely than
he, "O death, where is thy sting? O
grave, where is thy victory? The sting
of death is sin; and the strength of sin
is the law. But thanks be to God, which
giveth us the victory through our Lord
Jesus Christ."

As soon as the force of his disease
mitigated enough to allow him to leave

his bed, he began to visit and to take his place again in his pulpit and his prayer-meeting. When in his pulpit those who heard his sermons would scarcely know that he was an invalid; for his face was bright and his voice was strong and clear. One day he appeared in his pulpit after his sickness before an audience which filled his church to its utmost capacity. He preached with unusual fervor. His audience was greatly impressed. It seems to me no exaggeration to say that this one sermon converted more than a score of souls. But when he reached his home he was exhausted, and was obliged to take to his bed at once. He remained in an unconscious condition until the following noon. Sometimes he preached in Osaka, Tōkyō and Niigata, in the theaters, to audiences of several thousand people. The weakness of his lungs did not seem to impair the strength or clearness of his voice.

His sermons seemed almost equally

impressive for all classes of people, children as well as adults, unlearned as well as educated. For his knowledge and wisdom had come into his heart through his experience. I can refer to some results and ways of his sermons from his letters.

After preaching at the general conference of Osaka, he says in his letter to Mrs. Boutell, concerning his sermon from the text, "Notwithstanding in this rejoice not, . . . but rather rejoice, because your names are written in heaven" (Luke 10 : 20) : "God helped me in the preaching and many of the church members shed tears while I was preaching."

Of other services he says : "I preached a week ago last Sunday evening from text 'God is love.' After the service many of the audience expressed of their impression and effects. I preached last Sunday from Romans 15 : 3 : 'For even Christ pleased not himself.'"

"Mr. Leavitt has his Bible class after

our Sunday-school and has a good audience, and I interpret for him."

St. Barnabas Hospital,
Osaka, Japan, February 9, 1885.

Dear Mrs. Boutell, — I have been much better. The night sweat has stopped and I have gained in flesh. I preached the twenty-eighth of December the last to my people from the text, " Let us labour therefore to enter into that rest " (Heb. 4: 11), as I thought it would be an appropriate subject to preach on that day, being the last rest day of the year. And again the first Sabbath of this year from the often used text, " Fight the good fight of faith, lay hold on eternal life." When I preached the latter sermon the Rev. Mr. Morimoto, the editor of Fukuin Shimpō, being present at my church, took note of the sermon and published it in his paper, and when that paper came to one of my church members, who has been living at a distance, he was greatly pleased to hear my sermon again after so long a time.

But I caught cold that Sunday and was obliged to shut myself in the hospital nearly five weeks. I went out yesterday to preach the communion sermon from the text, " A new commandment I give unto you, that ye love one another."

Before I went out yesterday one of the nurses remarked to me that I must be shut in many weeks again if I did go out to preach, but this time I did not catch cold and feel no worse for my work of yesterday.

He speaks about the conversion of some children from his sermon : —

Among the children of our deacons there was one girl of nine years of age. One evening after she had heard a sermon she retired to her bed in the next room to that in which her parents slept. At about midnight her father heard some noise in her room that showed that she was not asleep. Therefore he almost scolded her for spending the night in some pleasure without sleeping, for it was now about midnight. She said: "Papa, I cannot sleep, for if I should, I might die before morning, and I am condemned as a sinner." Her father then saw that she was under conviction of sin. At first he was much perplexed as to what to do, for though he was an experienced deacon he had not often seen such deep conviction of sin in children. So he asked her what had been her sins, and she confessed. He then pointed her to the Lamb of God, who taketh away the sins of the world — as well as he could. They prayed together, and she consecrated herself to God that night.

As she received the truth at once, her fears left her, and she became calm and slept peacefully the rest of the night.

The father told his wife and together they were much impressed, feeling that God was in their house. The next day the father came to me to ask what it was best to do, for this was the first instance of the awaking of so young a child in our midst. I advised him to bring his daughter to be examined for admission to the Church.

Before being received into the Church she was invited to the house of a schoolmate to take dinner with them. The father of this family was the principal editor of a leading newspaper of the city, and had been educated in England. He was a well-educated man and an infidel. He allowed no kind of worship in his family. Our little girl knew this, and thought that if this unbelieving family should see her ask a blessing upon the food that was set on her little table, they would scoff at her; so she decided to ask her blessing in silence and none would know about it. Then her conscience troubled her with the thought that she had been ashamed

to confess the Saviour who had done so much
for her before men. So, though the dinner was
very fine, she ate it in bitterness and sorrow.
As soon as dinner was over she left, without
staying to play with the children, but went
right home with a heavy heart. She did not as
usual tell her parents of the fine feast that she
had attended.

Soon her father suspected that something was
wrong, and he asked his little daughter what
she had done, and she confessed all and how
she was ashamed to acknowledge Christ before
those worldly people. Then they kneeled together and she confessed her sin before God.
Soon after she was received into the Church,
and she is now a good and happy girl.

In connection with this same deacon, who
was a druggist, I will give you an account of
another remarkable conversion: —

One night one of his clerks, a young man of
eighteen or nineteen years of age, came in
great distress and earnestness to him to know
what he should do to escape the wrath to come.
The deacon, seeing the great earnestness of the
young man, was perplexed, and said to him:
" You are in great earnest, and if I should not
direct you right, it would be a great pity. We
have a pastor, and you would better wait till

to-morrow and see him." The young man said: "You cannot assure me that I will live until to-morrow."

The deacon knew that the pastor, who was in feeble health, had held an evening service and was sorry to have to arouse him in the dead of the night; but as he could not guarantee another day's probation, he hired a jinrikisha and sent the young man to the pastor's home. He came to me and the first words he said were the very words of the jailer of Philippi: "What must I do to be saved?" I directed him with a few words and in the simplest way possible to Christ, and that he should cast himself upon him. We prayed together, and he went home with a different heart, and ever since he has proved the reality of the change by a life of earnest work for Christ.

I will next give you an account of the conversion of several girls. On a Sunday afternoon a sermon was preached from Heb. 3:7, 8: "Therefore the Holy Ghost says, To-day if you will hear his voice, harden not your heart." That evening there was evidence of an awakening among the girls of our boarding school. Next morning I received a letter from one of the lady teachers, Miss Gardiner or Miss Colby, saying that several of the girls were under con-

viction of sin, and were unable to pursue their
duties and wanted to see me. She hoped that
I would come and assist in directing them
toward the light. I went, and calling one by
one those who were thus awakened, did what I
could to show them the way of salvation in
their several conditions, and prayed with each
one. All these girls, of ages from ten to fifteen
years, have since united with different churches
in Osaka.

Mr. Sawayama wrote to the writer at
one time about his work at Sanda, a country church, which shows us another fea-
ture of his preaching : —

While I was at Arima two deacons of Sanda
church came to me and asked me to preach
there. I asked about the condition of the
church, and they said that the work of God was
declining and all Christians were sleeping. I
went there last Friday and I preached that
night. Next morning the acting pastor called
on me and he asked me to preach to unchristians from that day. The reason why
he expressed such a desire was that the sermon
which I preached reflected very severely upon
them. Therefore they wanted me to preach to

unchristians, as they had some feeling against
the truth. I answered that I preach the truths
of the Bible; and I think the sermons must
be impressive to Christians as well as to unchristians. Therefore I cannot preach such a
sermon as to make an impression only on unchristians. If unchristians read the Bible, they will
fear and repent, and if Christians study it, they
will advance in their virtues. And I explained
to him about the true preaching. Then he was
impressed and confessed the convictions which
he had had since he heard my first sermon.
And he confessed his selfishness and sins, and
he said he is unworthy, not only to be acting
pastor but to be a church member. Therefore
he wished to resign his pastorship and membership, and he would join the church again
after his true conversion; and he shed many
tears. Then the deacons repented with tears,
and ladies also confessed their sins and sur-
rendered all things to God. I preached and
held prayer-meetings during a week, and many
were converted. I thought I would stay there
longer, but I was obliged to leave there to
look after some publishing.

And yet his deeds were more powerful
than his words. Many came to his bedside

to comfort him: all received from him
such courage and inspiration that he was
even more than ever a power in his church.
I myself visited him at the hospital often,
making the trips from a distant mission
field for the purpose of bringing him comfort in his illness. But he needed no
comfort; indeed he gave to me, I thought,
infinitely more than I gave to him. Just
before I left him he raised his heavy body
and took from the bureau his one cloak
and handed it to me, asking me to give it
to a poor Christian brother in the place
where I was preaching. Lately Mr. Nakaye, my intimate friend, wrote me about
a similar act. He says : —

"I called on Mr. Sawayama in the hospital with my friend some time in the year
1886. When we left him he handed us
an *awase* (a Japanese long dress which
can easily be remade into a lady's cloak),
and said to us: 'I heard that Mrs. ——,
(who is a widow and has several children) has been absent from church quite

often. I suppose she wants a new dress, but she cannot buy one, as she is poor; therefore she does not attend church often, from the sense of shame. Will you please, dear brethren, bring this to that lady and tell her to make a new dress of this and attend church?"

"I think," Mr. Nakaye continues, "those who received more love and attentions from him were the poor and lowest class. Who does not know this duty? But how many ministers practiced this truth as Mr. Sawayama did?"

I remember many such cases in which he seemed absolutely to forget his own illness in thinking how he could help some one else. At one time he wrote to a sick lady from his sick bed thus: "I have deep sympathy with you; but as it says in the Bible, 'Everything works for good,' everything is for the glory of God, profit of our soul, and happiness of the future life. Therefore we are very happy to trust in the hand of God, saying, 'Not as I will, but as thou wilt.'"

He was a man of prayer and devotion. He believed that everything, in God's providence, was working to perform the will of God. He prayed with a simple faith. Almost childlike in his trust, he seemed never to doubt that his prayer would be fulfilled. One day he expected to go to the mission field of his Naniwa Church, but he had no money. He told nobody his need, but, having prayed that he might have money enough to enable him to make the visit, he went on at his work, seemingly with an entire confidence that the need would be met. Very late that night a poor Christian woman came to him and handed him some money, saying that she had earned it unexpectedly that day and wanted to offer it for the mission work. A little later another came in with another contribution.

Mr. Sawayama was thankful, as he always was, but he was not surprised; it was just what he had expected; how otherwise? He went to the mission field, paid all his expenses, and returned, finding that the gift had just equaled his expenditure.

Rev. Mr. Miyagawa, who is one of the first graduates of Dr. Neesima's institution, pastor of one of the churches of Osaka, and one of the leaders of the religious movement in Japan, writes in The Christian, of Tōkyō, referring to Mr. Sawayama's prayers, as follows (translation) : —

I have noticed that while Mr. Sawayama was pastor of the Naniwa Church there existed a strong union in the church, and they undertook mission and educational work with enthusiasm; also that they went ahead of all other churches with the banner of independence and self-support, and that when their representatives appeared at the annual conference of Kumi-ai churches they insisted upon the duty of self-support with a burning spirit which seemed to move the whole meeting so that nobody could withstand it. I thought secretly that Mr. Sawayama must have been at work in all the affairs

of the church very busily from early morning
to late at night every day, feeling the shortness
of the time; but when I came to the church of
Osaka, which was situated near by his church,
I learned that he had had consumption for a
long time and had been obliged to lie on his
sick bed about two thirds of the year, and that
he could not attend to the large part of the
affairs of the church.

Then the following questions arose in my
mind and I could not answer them for a long
while; namely, With what kind of magnetic
power can he manage his church so successfully
all the time? Can he move his church members
as he can control his fingers by his will, by the
skillfulness of conversation and social excellency,
as he is a Yamaguchian [1]; or does he attract all
people by his amiable manners? But when he
departed from us we found a list of the names
of his church members, by which he used to pray
to our Father for individual members every
morning and evening, sometimes shedding
bloody tears. This list must have been kept
for many years, because it was stained with his
much handling. In some parts the letters were
indiscernible, it was so black. I thought, This

[1] The Japanese people regarded the people of Yamaguchi
province as a gracious, social people.

much-used list is a monument telling of his appeal to the Father for every member of his church by name. From this also I received the answer to all my questions concerning him, that the secret of his success was in prayer.

Mr. Sawayama says in his letters: — " I am now sick in the hospital, so I cannot work much; but I am praying constantly and the work of my church is blessed. Please pray for my work, which is God's."

" My great joy of yesterday was that I found in the church a lately backsliding man for whom I have been praying much. When the service was over I went straightway to speak a few loving words to him with much joy in my heart, though I could not exchange words with others, as the time was late and I ought to be back to the hospital very quickly; and I said to myself in heart, ' He was lost and is found.' "

A young man for whom Mr. Sawayama was praying was converted as follows, as reported in one of his letters: —

A young man in the employ of another of our deacons decided to leave his place. He had no good reason for doing so, and was trying to get away from Christian influence, as his conscience seemed to be troubling him. His Christian friends urged him not to go, but in spite of all he left, and went away seeking employment elsewhere. He soon fell in with an old friend whom he had not met for years, and before long told him that he wanted work. "Come with me," said his friend; "I know a good place for you."

He went to his friend's lodging, but in the night several policeman entered, making several arrests and closing the house. The poor young man found himself in jail under arrest for gambling, and his friend proved to be a gambler and the house where he had stopped a gambling house.

In the morning some food was brought to him, and as had been the custom at the house at Osaka he bowed his head in thanksgiving to God. He also prayed most earnestly that God would deliver him from the prison. He acknowledged that he knew these sufferings were sent him for having tried to run away from his duty; that he now humbled himself before God and was ready to follow wherever he might lead him.

Soon after he was taken before a policeman, who questioned him. The young man said he knew nothing of the business of his friend, as he had come from Osaka but the day before, and that while he was in Osaka he was in the employ of a Christian and that he surely was not a gambler. When he said he had been in a Christian family, the policeman said, "I can soon tell whether you are telling the truth or not, as I know something of the Christian work in Osaka. Where is the —— church?" To this the young man replied correctly. "Who is its pastor? Where is —— church and who is its pastor?" etc. The young man showed by his replies that he knew all about them. He was therefore released and came back to Osaka a penitent man, full of thanksgiving to God for so plainly showing him his duty. He is still a very earnest Christian.

Mr. Sawayama was very fond of praying with two or three brethren, and the prayer-meeting was a great delight to him. His mind and his body were equally active. If he could pray with some one, he would come down from his sick bed and kneel by a chair. Sometimes prayer-meetings were

held early in the morning. He attended
like an entirely well man. The prayer-
meetings in his church were therefore
always well attended and always enthusiastic. During the revival they were as
large as the Sunday congregations. When
Mr. Sawayama was very seriously sick,
prayer-meetings were held for him; and I
recall how all were so moved that no one
could trust his voice to speak.

Mr. Sawayama's principle in regard to
contributions — not merely his *maxim* but
his *principle* — was, " It is more blessed to
give than to receive." He held that the
accompaniment of the thankful spirit was
an essential part of giving; and that his
church might never give from a sense of
obligation or of shame, but from a thankful heart, he never persuaded or even
asked anyone to give. He was himself a
very methodical man, and gave two tenths
of his income to the church every month;
he also gave one tenth of all the gifts
which he had received from his friends

during his illness. This spirit could not but influence his church, and they offered more than one tenth with thankful hearts. No member ever complained of the burden of self-support; all were courageous and confident. The giving capacity of the church increased wonderfully. Many increased greatly the proportion of their contributions with the increase in their incomes. I remember one man who in the beginning could offer but sixty cents a month, which was one tenth of his income; but at the end of five years he gave twenty dollars a month. Another could offer at first only fifty cents a month; at the end of five years he gave fifteen dollars every month. But Mr. Sawayama's ideas and methods will appear more fully in his speech.

And not only did he know the way of giving, but he knew also how to receive and how to thank, as the following letters will show.

To Mrs. Boutell : —

OSAKA, October 7, 1878.

I have received twice your kind letters since I have been married, which inform me that you are going to send some presents to us for our home comforts. By receiving this news, how much I felt grateful to you all and to God who gave me such kind friends as you are, I cannot express. I have forsaken all and followed the Lord in putting myself in this position. . . . Great self-denial is necessary and I determined to follow the steps of the Lord, who on earth " had not where to lay his head," and so I could not have much comfort in this life, I thought; therefore what a grateful thing to me these presents of my friends are you can imagine. I have not yet received the box, but when I shall receive it I will write to the friends to thank you all and tell them more thoroughly about the condition of my life and household, etc. I am now waiting anxiously for the box.

Mrs. Boutell, I would like to thank you in this connection for the things of which you made me presents while I was at your home. Shirts, coats, drawers, and other things have been exceedingly useful to me. Since I came back I have not bought anything and of course I had no means to buy. All these things your presents supplied, and many of them will last all my life, I think, if the Lord will take me before very many years. To these add the presents of this time, we shall be very comfortable.

To Mrs. Packard : —

OSAKA, November 18, 1878.

A few weeks ago we received the box of many presents from ladies. I thank you for the beautiful book which you sent us with them. When we received the book I read it, together with my wife, and we talked to each other about the vanity of this world and the blessedness of Christ's abiding with us, and thanked God in our hearts that by the grace of God we are now what we are. The book is now on our parlor table and it is admired by all who come to see it as well as by us daily. I ask you to thank for us the church for the money which they gave us. It will help us in a great many ways to get our comforts for the Lord's work.

To Mrs. Boutell : —

OSAKA, February 10, 1880.

Mr. De Forest received fifty dollars from you as the gift from your church to me. I always feel very grateful for the thousand kindnesses of you and the friends there. I enclose the letter to the church to thank them for the money. This much money came to me so unexpectedly in the time of necessity, as I feel, and I told the church members the other evening, as though it was manna from heaven.

To Mrs. Boutell : —

OSAKA, November 2, 1884.

Thank you very much for forwarding five-dollar note, which Mrs. E. L. Brown kindly sent for me enclosed in your letter. I thank Mrs. Brown very much that she should remember me in that way.

To Mr. and Mrs. Packard: —

OSAKA, April 12, 1881.

I take opportunity to send you a *tetsubin* or iron teakettle by Mr. Leavitt, who is going back to America with his family. Tetsubin is one of the most popular things in Japanese homes of the middle class upward. They think that it is almost necessary thing for their own enjoyment and also entertainment of others. If you should enter a Japanese house, you will tetsubin find always over charcoal fire and water boiling in it. They make tea all the time with the water for themselves and others who may call on them.

I present this to you, as you might use this on

your table, when you take tea or coffee. The
form of the kettle itself is meant as a piece of
rock and crabs are on the face of both sides,
climbing up of the rock; rough bottom of the
inside of the kettle is purposely made for
musical sound when the water is boiling in it.
For keeping it nice, please throw water occasionally all over the face of kettle when it is very
hot, so that the water might instantly dry away.
By this way you could keep the color of the iron
looking nice. Never rub it hard with anything.
At first, the water boiled in it may have iron
taste, but it will be good by-and-by.

Mr. Sawayama was, withal, a man of
childlike simplicity and great humility. He
never disputed with anyone. He met with
much decided opposition in his methods of
self-support; but if at any time he could
not avoid expressing his convictions, he
expressed them in such a gentle manner
that no one cared to enter into controversy
with him. He was so truly humble that
he never criticized others. In the following letter the reader will see how humble
he was before God and men.

To Mrs. Naruse (translation) : —

OSAKA, January 11, 1885.

I thank you for your kind letter and I am very glad to know that your faith, love, and patience are increasing. I have read your letter several times and given thanks and prayed. I ought to have answered at once, but as the weather grows colder my breathing becomes more difficult; so I have delayed to take my pen. But I preached on the last Sunday of last year and I was able to preach again on the first Sunday of this year, so I am not very badly off.

You wrote me about the deepness of your sins and your unworthiness to serve God. I think this is one sign of the increase of the grace of God. I will tell you of one or two of my experiences through which I have passed since the attack of last year. Last October, while I was sick in bed, I felt the coldness of my love to God and to my brethren, and I was very sorry. And I prayed that my love might be increased.

Though I expected that God would make my love to him and to the brethren burn in my heart contrary to my hope, I only felt the deepness of my sin and my inferiority to my brethren. So after I had had this feeling for a time I realized that "I am the chief of sinners."

And at the same time I understood that it was
not only in the experience of humility that St.
Paul said, "I am the chief of sinners," but he
felt it was really so. From this time I was impressed especially with the greatness of the
grace of God toward such a sinner as I am,
the chief sinner, and I esteemed and valued
very highly my brethren as I saw their worthi-
ness, goodness, and righteousness. Thus my
adoration and love toward God and my brethren
increased and my heart was filled with good and
pleasant thoughts.

So you see my mistake. At first I could not
understand the answer of God to my prayers.
If the feeling of love to God and to my brethren had burned in my heart, it would have dis-
appeared very soon, as it was only feeling. But
my experience was not a vain feeling, but based
on firm reason, because my love to God increased
from the knowledge of the deepness of my sins
and the greatness of the grace and love of God.
And as to the love of the brethren, this burned
more deeply because of my honor and respect
for their virtues. Then I was impressed with
those words which Christ spoke: " Wherefore
I say unto you, her sins, which are many, are
forgiven; for she loved much; but to whom little
is forgiven, the same loveth little" (Luke 7 : 47).

And the other day, having been reading the Revelation, I found at many places the word *repent* in the second and third chapters. I thought that these words were spoken to those who sinned or became cold after their conversion and some of them had committed great sins; but God promised to give his grace to them if they would repent, even such sinners. So I can believe surely that we can receive his remission of sins which are committed after conversion, if we truly repent, though they are terrible things and we doubt the remission even after repentance. In the early morning of the first of last December, as soon as I awaked, I met a temptation of the devil. He said to my heart: "Paul, do you not remember that you were lying in this hospital last December too? You have spent almost all of your time this year in the hospital on this sick bed and you have not been at work for God but have only been lying down here. What do you think of this day? Is it not the first day of December? You say you have sacrificed yourself to God, but you have not attended to your church and have not preached. Don't you feel sorry? See the other pastors! They are working successfully for the propagation of the kingdom of God."

Thus i began to feel very sad; but very soon

good tidings came to my mind through the Holy Ghost because of these words of Christ (Luke 10 : 17–20), when the seventy returned with joy because of their success in preaching: Jesus said: "Rejoice not in this," which is changeable according to the conditions of life, but "rather rejoice because your names are written in heaven." This idea drove away immediately the temptation of the devil and I thought with glad feelings that I am an unworthy servant; but by the great mercy of the Father I was born into the kingdom of heaven and I am now a citizen of that kingdom and no one can take from me this joy.

The happiness in this world.

"Surely goodness and mercy shall follow me all the days of my life."

The happiness in the future world.

"I will dwell in the house of the Lord for ever" (Ps. 23: 6).

At one time Mr. Sawayama had been praying for a revival. It did not come. He imagined that the fault was in himself, so he consecrated himself anew to his work. After this experience he addressed a woman's meeting, in which the interest

at once became so great that it was turned
into an inquiry meeting. Many went
away and related their experience to
others. This was the beginning of a
revival. All the students in the girls'
school were converted and began new
lives.

Mr. Sawayama held a prayer-meeting
and a preaching service every day. The
church was always filled. After the sermon there would be an inquiry meeting.
This was the first religious revival in
Japan. At this time I tried to write to
the Christian paper an account of this
movement, but Mr. Sawayama would not
allow me to do so. He shrank from anything which resembled praise.

Notwithstanding his strong revivalistic
spirit, his methods in revivals were above
reproach. He never urged people, he
never scolded about people's sins, he never
made people feel uncomfortable by employing artifices to induce them to confess their sins. His conduct at such times,

and indeed always, was natural and quiet,
with an element of dignity. He could
accommodate himself, apparently without
effort, to all kinds of people.

CHAPTER IV.

HOME MISSION WORK; HIS SPEECH AT THE GREAT CONFERENCE.

MR. SAWAYAMA'S persistent example gradually influenced many Japanese churches. The most of the Congregational (or Kumi-ai) churches are self-supporting, and many of other denominations. Mr. Sawayama also insisted that this same principle should extend to the Home Mission work, but in this he was not seconded by the majority; so the Home Mission work is supported in part by the native churches and in part by the American Board.

Mr. Sawayama says in his letter about the beginning of the Japanese Home Missionary Society : —

"On the second and third of February, 1878, we had a general church conference in the girls' school of Osaka. In this

conference we formed the Home Missionary Society, and Mr. Neesima and Mr.
Imamura, of Kobé, and myself were appointed as committee to manage the entire
affairs of the society."

The mission work was divided into two
departments: that which was carried on
in fields remote from the churches, and
the local mission of each church. The
rule was followed that the more remote
fields should draw eight tenths of their
support from the American Board and
two tenths from the native churches; the
expenses of the local missions were paid
in a different proportion, six tenths by the
Board and four tenths by the native
churches.[1] But Mr. Sawayama's church
did not receive any pecuniary aid whatever from the Board from the beginning.

The local mission field of the Naniwa
Church was the province of Yamato.
One of his church members, who decided

[1] But now about half is paid by the native churches, and
the other half by the American Board. The proportion
varies from year to year.

in the revival to become a preacher, began
his preaching there. He preached several
times in the theater of Koriyama city.
Many were interested. One man in particular was much impressed, but he shared
the doubts and suspicions which almost
all the people felt toward the work. He
thought that perhaps the preacher was
preaching for the sake of money; so he
tested him in various ways. He invited
him to dinner at his home to test whether
he was selfish or not. He called on him at
his lodgings to find out his private conduct.
He found that the preacher received no
money except for his expenses, and that he
was supported entirely by native Christians.
His prejudices were removed. He was surprised at the self-sacrificing spirit of the
preacher and the native Christians, who
had sent him there. Soon afterwards he
became a Christian and began to offer
something for the work.

At the same time one old lady became
a very good Christian, and gave much

money for the church and its benevolent
work. She helped very many of the
poorer people. After about one year a
church of thirty members was organized.
A house was bought and was rebuilt to
meet the purposes of a church. All the
members contributed money and work.

As soon as the work was completed,
some hater of Christianity wrote some
insulting words on the white wall of the
church. They were written in large letters and were spread over every blank
space between the windows, as if they
had been the motto of the church. The
Christians did not erase them.

Mr. Sawayama makes mention in a letter
of an incident that occurred in this town : —

Among the converts in that place was a carpenter and his wife, both very earnest, but unlearned people. One evening while the wife
was preparing supper she tried to read her
New Testament, but finding great difficulty she
said to herself: "There is a precious treasure in
this book, and the Almighty God could give me

power in some way to understand this book." So she kneeled down in her kitchen and prayed aloud. The house was very small, and a traveler passing by heard her earnest prayer and was much impressed and came in and asked to whom she was speaking. She told him that she was a Christian and was praying to the Christian God. While she was telling him about her faith her husband came home from work and they both told him of the Way.

He then confessed to them that he had hated Christianity and that he was the head of a band who were planning to break up the meetings of Christianity in his city, Nara, two and one-half miles distant. He appeared to be much impressed by what he heard from these humble people regarding their faith in Christianity. While we have not heard anything further from him, yet we know that the meetings in Nara have been held undisturbed from that time to this, and we have lately had increased interest in the work there.

Nara was the capital of Japan in ancient times, and many places and buildings there are connected with historical incidents, and its *Daibutsu,* or great bronze image, is also a very famous thing.

This lady, wife of the carpenter, mastered enough of the written language to read the Bible and to write letters in the Japanese character through her enthusiastic study in her kitchen for a long while. And her husband worked for many days without any wages to build our church.

Koriyama was the center of the mission work in the province of Yamato. At this time the Buddhist and Shintō priests were greatly enraged against Christianity, as were the people also. The priests sought in every town and village to destroy Christianity. I will refer to a few instances, that the reader may see the condition of the mission work.

One day a preacher and two Christian brethren went from the city into a town to preach. They had secured a crowded audience, when ten Buddhist priests and many young men came in. After the preaching the priests began to dispute with the Christians. Their purpose was to excite the people and if possible make an attack upon the Christians. But the latter were so calm, and answered them so discreetly that they found it hard to make an opportunity for the attack. When their anger was almost breaking forth, policemen came in and offered their protection to the preacher and his companions.

Several of this audience became Christians, partly because they were impressed with the truth which the preacher spoke, but more because of their admiration for the spirit and character of the Christians. One of those who were converted was a Shintō priest[1]. He was an earnest man, and displayed to the people the truth of Christianity and the errors of Shintōism. He resigned his priesthood and returned his degree to the government. But the people were very angry with him and drove him from his house.

Another of the converts was a young man whose conversion was extremely

[1] He came to the meeting to protest against Christianity, but he found truth.

odious to his family. During a call which the preacher made upon him his grandmother came into the room and stood watching them. The preacher bowed according to the Japanese custom, but the old lady did not respond by a word or even a sign. The preacher attempted to speak to her, but she covered her ears with her hands. After the preacher had gone the old lady threw the teakettle at her grandson, and threw his Bible and all his other religious books into the fire.

The persecution of another young man was more disagreeable, not to say severe. The anger of his parents was almost without restraint. He would sometimes be struck with a hoe or some similar implement. At other times he was pushed out of his house in entire nakedness in the winter night. When he was intending to go to the church to receive baptism, and had gone into the store to get his cloak, his mother locked the door from the outside. When matters had come to such a

pass that it was really dangerous for him
to stay longer at home he ran away, and
did not return for a year. I knew a girl
whose relations with her parents and
family were entirely cut off for many
years, so that she could not even return to
her home. But in these and many other
cases none of those who had been converted lost their Christian faith.

This was the condition in which the
mission work in the province of Yamato
was begun.

I will here give the speech, which I have
already mentioned several times, which
Mr. Sawayama delivered before the Inter-
Denominational Missionary Conference in
Osaka in May, 1881, on " The Self-support
of the Japanese Native Church " : —

I am one of those who believe that the church
to which I belong has received special blessing,
owing to the fact that from the time of the
founding of our church stress has been laid
upon the idea of self-support. And although
personally I have had little more than six years'

experience in the working of the system, yet I am desirous of offering for the consideration of the conference now assembled for the purpose of discussing this subject the results of my experience.

To express my own conviction on this subject, I would say that self-support (1) is in accordance with the teaching of Scripture; (2) is beneficial to the church; (3) that if the church will in faith endeavor to carry out the principle, it will be found by no means unattainable.

We will take these three branches of my subject in order: —

1. *The support given to the theory of self-support by the teaching of Scripture.*

Men of the world, in accomplishing anything they set themselves to do, resort to certain means. If we look at the matter now before us from the standpoint of ordinary human reason, it is very apparent that the duties of believers in Christianity are for the most part such as spring from faith; and the performance of these duties that proceed from faith constitutes what we call the doing of the will of God, and affords the proof that we believe his promises. It is only when this condition is fulfilled that the blessing upon which so much depends will be vouchsafed. If we look at things in

the light of human reason, however great the
present difficulties may be, those who are versed
in the teaching of Scripture should act in
accordance with this teaching without the slight-
est misgiving. This it is that is spoken of as
" walking by faith and not by sight," and only
when a believer has this kind of faith does he
begin to be capable of doing work that is pleasing to God, and only then is he in a position to
receive God's help; for " without faith it is
impossible to please God." Faith then, and
faith alone, is the source from which the Church
derives a true spirit of self-support.

If we refer to the New Testament, we do not
find that Christ on the occasion of sending evangelists out to preach the gospel assisted them
by means of money. And in reference to those
churches which were founded by the apostles,
although we find instances of the theory of self-
support being acted upon by them, we never
find cases in which the opposite theory is re-
sorted to. In point of fact, although we find
that Paul collected money from churches that
had been recently organized for the purpose of
assisting his own countrymen, we never read that
the opposite of this was done; namely, that the
new churches were assisted financially by the
older ones. In fact, so established a custom

was it for the churches to advance money for the purpose of assisting the apostles in their work, that we find Paul asking for forgiveness for not being burdensome to the Corinthian church (2 Cor. 12: 13); that is, for not asking for pecuniary help from them.

It is clear enough, then, without further discussion, that the principle of self-support was the one acted on in the early Church.

In the Old Testament also we find that the rich and poor alike paid tithes to God, and subscribed toward the maintenance of the priests and for the keeping up of the service of the temple.

Seeing then that the principle of self-support is one of the great agencies of the church, we believe that the subscription of rich and poor alike for the maintenance of the church is specially pleasing to God.

2. *The benefits to the church ensured by the adoption of this plan.*

As believers are bought with a price, from the day of their repentance and belief nothing they possess is their own, but is all sacred to God, to whom it is presented. On knowing, then, what the will of the Lord is, there should not be a thing that they possess that they are not ready to offer for the Lord's use; and they

should be led and taught to believe that it is
but proper that their possessions should be
handed over to the God of all riches. It is
for the most part by the use that people make
of money that the nature of their hearts is
known; by the use of their money they influence their hearts for either good or evil. In
the Bible it is said: "The love of money is the
root of all evil" (1 Tim. 6: 10); again, "Make to
yourselves friends of the mammon of unright-
eousness" (Luke 16: 9). If there is anything
that is very much bound up with the purposes
of God in my heart, I shall pay special attention
to the work of impressing upon believers the
claims of this thing. The principle of self-
support, being among believers the outcome of
faith, affects seriously the whole work of the
church. We cannot therefore agree with those
who treat the whole subject of financial dependence or independence as though it were merely
a pecuniary matter of small moment to the
church. As such persons, however, are to be
found, I shall now proceed to state what advantages to the church are to be derived from the
principle of self-support.

Paul said: "If we have sown unto you spiritual things, is it a great thing if we shall reap
your carnal things?" (1 Cor. 9: 11). According

to the principle laid down here, the believer, having received a gift of more value than all the treasure of the world, should gladly give his carnal things for the Lord's service. If in the very commencement of missionary work this is not emphasized, it is to be feared that gradually the great grace manifested in man's salvation will be forgotten, and that believers will not value as they should that state of bliss to which they are called. The principle of self-support, then, is the one thing that is instrumental in making each believer mindful of the Lord's grace and the blessedness of his salvation. The faith that men have is manifested by means of money, and therefore if from the commencement people be urged to give money toward the support of the work of God, a spirit of self-denial will be produced; but if the contrary be the case, they will gradually lose heart in the work and grow to be mean and ignoble. This being so, those who object to giving money are sure to be persons of weak faith on to the end, and at last will make shipwreck of the faith they have. Among those who have gone astray there are numbers like this. If from the very first the principle of self-support be insisted on, the different bodies of Christians will look upon their churches as their own, and will show great diligence in spreading the gospel; if they receive support from others, they will look on the Church as belonging to some one else and will grow remiss in Christian work.

I will take an extreme case : there is a church that is altogether supported by a foreign missionary. It happened that the church in which they worshiped was in want of a stove; seeing that the church itself had been put up by a foreign missionary, the members looked to him to provide the fittings required for the church; and as they regarded the whole matter as something for which they were in no way responsible, they let things go as they would till the foreign missionary advanced money to procure a stove, which was then handed over to the church members for them to put up. The next day some of them came to the missionary's house and said that they had spent time the day before in putting up the stove, and would not the missionary give them some remuneration? and of course all the fuel that was required for the stove was paid for by the foreign missionary. As a culmination of this state of things, the believers in this church looked upon the conversion of unbelievers as a work done for the benefit of the missionary.

Unless great care is taken, such believers as

these will entirely forget that their church work is a responsibility that God has laid upon them. If a church in time of distress and out of its poverty subscribes towards the support of its pastor, and by means of self-denial, the pastor too will deny himself and be ready to endure affliction for the sake of the church. The self-denial exercised by both parties will lead to their love for each other. When the opposite is the case, when the church does nothing towards supporting the pastor, it is to be feared that he will be looked upon by the people as a mere hireling; and he himself will be deficient in the spirit of self-denial. Thus that union of heart and combination of effort, that spirit of love which is so necessary to success, will be wanting.

Again, if by self-denial a church is able to give to God, and has the spirit that enables it with joy to endure affliction, then the pastors, evangelists, and missionaries who are supported by it will all feel that they are intimately connected with the carrying out of this principle, and that they follow in the footsteps of Him who denied himself and who had not where to lay his head. They will realize that they have a Father, who knows that they require the necessaries of life, and they will trust him and work with diligence and without distraction.

The principle of self-support, then, involves one's working in the way of faith in the promises, and means that one's poverty is supplied by the riches of Christ's grace; and although naturally this course will involve a number of difficulties, if in the midst of trouble we pray to the Lord for help, and renouncing self depend on him, we shall gradually get nearer to him, and our faith as a church will continually increase. The principle of self-support has a tendency to diminish the number of those lovers of the world who act the hypocrite when they enter the Church of Christ. What the real believer seeks for is not the pleasures of the world and the flesh, but the endless bliss of the life to come and only spiritual profit. He seeks to conquer himself and glorify God, and upon this alone he sets his mind. There are some rich believers in certain churches who object to subscribing money, and who say: " When we entered the Christian Church we did not suppose that, like those who belong to the Buddhist and Shintōist sects, we should constantly be called upon to give money for this and that; we entered the Church to economize in this respect, but we find that it is not so, and that as Christians we are still expected to subscribe money for various objects; we must say we are

disappointed in finding things as they are!" If
the idea of self-support had been acted on from
the first, such mistaken notions would never
have been entertained.

When, instead of teaching them to depend on
the principle of self-support, money is given to
believers, we are on the way to make them think
lightly of the Scripture which says, "Seek first
the kingdom of God and his righteousness, and
all other things shall be added unto you." We
are teaching them to doubt God's promises to
them, and to think that their work depends for
its success on money more than on the strength
of the promises. Thus the minds of believers
are gradually weakened (Matt. 6: 19–34).

The principle of self-support, then, is but an
acting up to that which Christ taught the rich
young man; namely, the giving up of all the
treasure and glory of this world and the accu-
mulating of treasure in heaven. If help is received from the foreign missionary and there is
no dependence on our own efforts, who will exercise self-denial and feel responsible for the
work of the church? We shall of course think
that there is no use in our troubling ourselves
over a thing for which other people are responsible. The benefits arising from evangelistic
work are such as affect the church, the evan-

gelists, and those who are members of the missionary committees, as well as the places in
which the work is carried on. If self-denial
be practiced, and money be subscribed by the
believers, the members will always be thinking
of mission work, and prayer will be offered on
its behalf; and although all will not be directly
engaged in the work, yet there will be a feeling of responsibility connected with it. Any
account of the circumstances under which it is
conducted, as well as the results that it yields,
will be listened to with pleasure and thankfulness. If evangelistic work be carried on more
diligently, there will be a correspondence between the outlay of money and the increase of
a spirit of self-denial in the church; and not
only this, but being a thing that concerns
themselves, the members of the church will
use discretion in the outlay of money.

On the one hand, then, there will be an exhorting of the evangelists to be more zealous in the
work; on the other hand, there will be a readiness to make known the circumstances of the
work. Thus the whole church will be stirred
up, and will seek to help the evangelists by
prayer, and to increase their zeal; and whilst
doing this they themselves will be brought
nearer to God. This spirit existing among the

evangelists themselves, and the members of the church, they will one and all be ready to deny themselves and do the will of God, and depend on the promises alone.

If those who are engaged in direct evangelistic work, and all the members of the church, have this spirit of self-denial and carry on the work in this spirit, those who receive the gospel will gradually lose their selfishness and will learn how to glorify God and push forward the evangelistic work in the places where it is being carried on.   This will be a means of producing in them genuine faith, and they will thus learn to deny themselves.   For in the practice of self-denial they will be very much guided by the conduct of other believers.   Thus when believers stimulate each other and assist each other, God's name will be glorified and spiritual blessings sought and received.

On the contrary, when money is received from foreigners there is great danger of all Christian zeal being lost.   I could give numerous instances of this that have come under my own notice, and I think they would not be without interest; but this would lengthen my address too much.

To state in a word the benefits to be derived from the carrying out of the principle on which

I have been insisting, they are as follows: —
Believers are by this means led to self-denial, and
spirit of independence and faith is promoted.
That each believer should have this spirit is
most essential to enable him to perform effi-
ciently those duties which devolve on each as a
Christian, as well as to conduce to the glory of
God. If the spirit of self-support yields so
much benefit to the individual Christian, it is
manifest how large an aggregate of good to the
whole Church will be produced by its general
adoption.

3. *A state of self-support is not unattainable.*

By self-support I mean the providing of
money by the Church for the carrying on of its
work; namely, the maintenance of the Japanese churches by the Japanese themselves; the
paying of the pastors and evangelists, and the
providing of such money as is required for the
due discharge of the duties of Christians. As
it is not the support of American churches or
of American teachers, there is nothing unrea-
sonable or impracticable in this.

The principle of self-support is a principle
that concerns all the members of the church,
and for which all alike are responsible; it is the
principle of all giving according to their means.
This is vastly important. There are many who,

for want of setting aside a regular time for giving and fixing the amount they intend to give, neglect giving altogether. The rich, for instance, may be able to give any amount; but because they do not fix on the exact amount· they will give, it often ends in their giving absolutely nothing. With the poor, although the circumstances are very different, the result is the same. They live from hand to mouth, and it is not likely that they will find any surplus money to give to the church if they are not in the habit of fixing the exact amount they intend to subscribe; and so it often happens that they subscribe neither cents nor mills.

It will be asked, How is the principle of self-support to be carried out? I reply that if all believers, whether rich or poor, were never to neglect giving a tenth of their earnings, there would be no difficulty about the matter. As regards other expenses of the church, each believer might every day, or week by week, lay by money for this purpose, and at the end of the month the expenses be divided up and each man take his share in defraying them according to his ability. In this case the poor would not have to advance much at one time, no one would feel the matter a burden, and yet the sum accumulated by degrees would

be considerable; and by means of it a great
deal of good could be accomplished. [For the
support of a girls' school the share of each sub-
scriber was two mills a day.] In our church
we are in the habit of giving one yen each
towards the repairs of the church every ten
months.

If the same plan be adopted in collecting
money to defray incidental expenses, there will
be little difficulty in meeting them. I have
been in the habit of exhorting my people from
the pulpit to give a tenth of their earnings.
There are members who not only do this but
who give for other objects also, as occasion calls
for it. Doubtless there will be some who will
not act up to this principle, but among members
of churches I doubt whether there is one who
would not give a certain amount every month.
I believe most of the members of churches feel
their responsibility in this matter.

There are those who say that although after a
church has become wealthy it is very proper to
enforce the law of self-support, at the present,
when there are many poor people in churches,
and when there are so many who find it difficult
to get a living, it is very wrong to insist on
their being self-supporting; for by doing this
you make the subscribing of money a source

of trouble to the members of the church, and prevent them from serving God with joy; and furthermore, by adopting such a course you weaken the faith of some persons. My experience is, as I have repeatedly said already, that the giving of money is the means of increasing the spiritual blessing received by believers, and therefore we may say that the giving of money tends to increase rather than decrease the joy which believers have in the service of God.

In the case of the Jews, when they had been commanded to give tithes of all they possessed and did not do it they were accounted robbers of God's property (Mal. 3:8). Jesus, when he saw that the poor widow in giving her mites was giving all that she had, praised her because out of her poverty she had given to God (Luke 21:1-4). Paul said of the Macedonians that out of their poverty they had sent to him, and that he rejoiced over the happy state of faith in which they were found, and commended them to God, who would supply all their need.

Thus it is plain that the giving of money in time of poverty is pleasing to God, as well as the means of bringing spiritual blessing to the donors themselves. God expects us to give only according to our ability and not of necessity either, but cheerfully; but this may be said not only in reference to the giving of money but in reference to everything connected with Christian duty.

If the church does not voluntarily entertain a regard for the plan of self-support, it is not to be supposed that it will carry it out well. The true believer will follow after righteousness as one that hungers and thirsts, and then he will deny himself and progress more and more in faith and zeal. He that stumbles in this matter stumbles because his heart is not right before God.

Again, there are those who say it is not good to insist on self-support just now, when the Church is still poor; wait until she becomes rich, say they, and then refuse all foreign help. It seems to me that when the Church advances and becomes far more wealthy than she is now, then her duties will have proportionately increased. This being so, the ease or difficulty of establishing a principle of self-support is immensely affected by the time at which it is attempted, whether now or later on. If it is difficult now, I fear that later on, when the churches shall have settled down into the condition of dependence, the difficulty will be still greater. At the present time, though the financial resources of the Church are very limited, the duties of the Church and the demands made on these resources are correspondingly limited. When I speak of the duties of the Church being limited, I refer to the fact that at present the number of believers is small, and that therefore even if there was a large sum of money at the disposal of the Church, there is not the means of using it just now that there will be when the number of believers is largely increased.

At the present time, how many men are there who may be looked on as real evangelists? To my mind just now the want of men should cause us more anxiety than the want of money. I was impressed with a remark made to this effect two or three years ago when some one said: "At the present time it is not the want of men that troubles us, but the poverty of the Church; if the Church possessed the means wherewith to pay good salaries, numbers would be ready to give up their present occupations and become evangelists." There may be times, for all I know, when such a principle as this is acted on, but I believe that in the case of those who believe in undertaking Christian work because they are called of God to do it, those are very few with whom money is such a supreme object as to lead them to doubt the promise that all necessary things shall be given them by God,

and who wait to see whether they will receive
good wages before they engage in Christian
work. In the case of those evangelists about
whose genuineness there is no doubt, who have
been called by God and the Church to undertake
the work, they will never allow their service to
God to depend on the presence or absence of
money; they will devote themselves and all
they possess to the work of spreading the gospel. God has promised that necessary things
shall be supplied; therefore the true minister
should wait for some church to provide the
money necessary for his support, and to employ
him. This is giving up all and following
Christ. This is following in the path of Peter,
John, and the other apostles who became ministers of God.

It is not simply an increase of men, without
regard to their qualification, that we need. If
we employ a number of men that are not real
evangelists, we shall find that they are not able
to do the work of Him who alone can save the
soul. Doubtless there will be a great saving of
time by having an increase in the number of
workers, and there will be other beneficial
results as well; yet it behooves us to take care
how we build the Church of God. If we build
with wood, hay, and stubble, such workman-

ship will be destroyed by fire at the last day, and we shall suffer loss; our works shall be tried in God's fire. Therefore that our work should be real and that we should make use of gold, silver, costly stones, material that will stand the trial of that day, is most important (1 Cor. 3: 12–15).

It is said by some that in our church in the matter of self-support we overdo the thing altogether; that we insist on the church being wholly self-supporting, and that in attempting to become so the believers have each to give too much money; that it is a source of great distress to them, and that they get no peace. But this is all a mistake. If there is any one in our church who finds the giving of money a source of trouble to him, it is because he has been remiss in doing his duty in this respect. Those who have learned how to give, those who believe our Lord's words and think it " more blessed to give than to receive " — these give with pleasure and without stint.

To give an instance of this: take the money that has been advanced for evangelistic purposes during the past two years. The monthly average has been ten yen, and the yearly average from 110 to 139 yen; yet on no occasion have I pressed a single person. Each one has presented to me what amount of money he thought proper, and when the sum has been insufficient I have prayed to God and he has given me more. There has been no requiring that each person shall pay so much, no forcing of any kind; nevertheless up to the present time there has been no want of money for the various branches of work. This is sufficient proof that the giving of money is not looked upon as a trial.

There are those who say that the carrying out of the principle of self-support is the means of bringing trouble on the Church, while God never designed it should suffer. I reply that we know of no trouble that has been brought on us by our own mistakes in this matter; but we do know that in denying ourselves we are following in the footsteps of Christ and endeavoring to act up to the spirit of Saint Paul, who buffeted his flesh, hoping thereby to be a partaker of more spiritual blessing.

There are those who think that unless in the church accounts a balance to the credit of the church is in hand, nothing whatever should be undertaken. My experience leads me to believe that where there is real work going on the means for carrying it on will be forthcoming. I do not mean to say that no difficulties whatever will occur; but if in trying to carry out

the principle of self-support we are doing the
will of God, then the Church will be benefited
by it, the believers will gain strength, their hope
will be made more fervent, and the way of
faith be advanced.   As an illustration of what
I said just now, that where there is real work
the money will be forthcoming, let me relate
what occurred last year: —

Owing to the work of evangelization having
made such progress, we thought it advisable to
employ a man who should do nothing else but
preach to the heathen.   Having found a man
of faith who seemed very suitable for the work,
we were desirous of employing him, but were
at a loss to know how to provide his salary.   This
difficulty was got over by the salary being provided by the believers belonging to the church.
Here is a case in which the worker and his
work are alike pleasing to God, and in which it
was felt that the evangelist was qualified for
his work; therefore the money for his support
was gladly advanced.

Again there are those who wish to do things
so precisely that, like merchants, they think that
unless money sufficient to meet all the expenses
is in hand at the commencement, although they
know the will of God, they cannot make any
attempt to carry it out.   Such as these, without

advancing far enough to ascertain what the
principle of self-support really is, meet half
way, and prophesy certain failure to the scheme;
and those who do this to show that the course
they recommend is in accordance with the will
of God are in the habit of referring to Luke
11:28, in which we are exhorted to count the
cost before commencing anything. But this
illustration, rather than supporting their argu-
ment, supports ours, for Christ here exhorts
those who serve him to continue to the end
denying themselves, bearing affliction, for this
is what they are to expect beforehand; and they
are exhorted to take care that they do not lose
heart and stumble. If such arguments as are
advanced by those of whom I am now speaking
were to be strictly maintained and acted upon,
it would soon end in the chief object of Christian
work, considered as a work that is to be origi-
nated by believers themselves, being lost sight
of altogether.

There are those who say, " Our church has
tried to support itself and failed; and having
proved it to be impracticable, we consider the
discussion of the question utterly useless." It
seems to me that it is the commencement of self-
support that shows what believers are made of.
If at that time Christians are ready to deny

themselves, and each takes his share in the responsibility of supporting the church, and if at the same time there is a spirit of unity among them, the plan will work.

When the opposite is the case, it must necessarily fail. The presence of this spirit in the church is intimately connected with the state of faith of those who belong to the church. Whilst listening to the remarks of various Christian brethren, I hear it continually said that as at present the financial resources of the Church are very limited, unless some rich people are brought into it, an attempt is made to accumulate church property, and means are devised for getting money, nothing can be done.

To hear these people talk it would seem as though they wished to attain financial independence without touching their own pockets. It is to be feared that such persons as these will lose the spirit of self-denial and the readiness to serve God as real believers ought to do. Christ said that whosoever could not give up everything for his sake was not worthy to be called his disciple. The great want of the church to-day is strong faith. If this faith be present, the money will be forthcoming.

Take an illustration of this: Here is a man walking by the sea, and he sees a man who has

fallen into the water. Either he will jump into
the water to save him or he will throw a rope
to him with the hope of saving him by this
means. If he has no rope, he will attempt to
save him by throwing his girdle [1] into the water.
This girdle may have cost some thirty or forty
yen; but does he grudge the money when his
brother's life is in danger? No; rather than
regret the loss of a costly girdle a man will rejoice that he has an opportunity of so using it.
If this is done with the object of saving a life
that must be taken away some day, how much
more should believers be ready to go to any expense that may be required if they really believe
that they will thus be able to save the life of an
immortal soul! As a matter of fact, does the
Church's lack of the money required for the
work of saving souls arise from there being
nothing in the possession of believers to give?
Is it not rather owing to the weak faith which
keeps them from giving?

There are those who say that if a church, with
a view of becoming self-supporting in everything, has to subscribe money for a large number
of objects, some most important things will have
to be neglected, and thus great injury be done
to the church. As for instance they say of the

---

[1] The Japanese girdle is very long.

Roka Church: "They are called a self-supporting church, but seeing that they do not possess a church building, in a most essential particular they are deficient: we look upon the possession of a place of worship as most indispensable to the carrying on of the work of the church, for in case of persecution arising and it proving impossible to hire a house, if there were no church, there would be no basis whatever for the carrying on of the work."

I think that if, like other bodies of Christians, we could erect a good-sized church, with an increased amount of light and purer air when we meet, it would be most helpful to our work as well as pleasant in itself; but at the same time we do not think this has anything to do with a church's being deemed entirely self-supporting. A self-supporting church is a church that pays its teachers, pastors, and evangelists, and provides funds for the propagation of the gospel. These things are of primary importance. But in reference to the matter of erecting a building to be set apart for worship, if there be a desire on the part of the church to put up such a building, the means of erecting it will be forthcoming. And as regards a time of persecution coming, in which any house hired for preaching would have to be given up, at such a

time the church would be in as much danger of
being set on fire as the house is of being taken
away. At such times we must leave our cause
in the hand of the Almighty, and there will be
no occasion for anxiety. At the time of the
apostles it seems that church buildings were not
numerous. As we read of "the church which
is in his house," it appears that houses were
used as churches. Therefore it cannot be said
now that because a house is hired and used as a
church a church is not self-supporting.

I have heard it said that when a church like
mine carries out the law of self-support to the
extent of conducting the various branches of
the work without receiving any pecuniary help
from foreign missionary societies, such a church
is bigoted or that it is desirous of making for
itself a name. It is nothing of the kind. Our
only desire is that the principle of self-support
be strictly observed, for if even on only one
occasion or in some small matter help be received from some one else, the believers' sted-
fastness of purpose becomes relaxed and they
lose the spirit of zeal; and we fear lest its
effects should be felt throughout the whole
Church; and as our natures are weak we take
precautions against our going astray in this
matter.

Seeing that there is a good number of brethren in our church who do not at all like to have the principle of self-support observed, and wishing to follow the will of God in the matter, I have prayed earnestly about it and have carefully examined myself in reference to it; but it is plainly my duty to follow what I consider to be the truth.

I have set forth, then, before you all the arguments that have led me to believe in the principle of self-support. I hope that you will thoroughly discuss the subject. I and my church, seeing that we belong to Christ, whatever can be in accordance with his will, that we will follow. If we can be brought to believe that any other way than that we have walked in is in accordance with his will, we will reform and walk in that way.

I hope you will all state your convictions on the subject without any reserve whatever.[1]

[1] I should attribute the merit of stirring up the spirit of self-reliance, self-help, and self-support in Japanese society and in Japanese churches in the main to Samuel Smiles, Rev. H. H. Leavitt, and Rev. Paul Sawayama. They were the champions of the principle of self-support there. "Self-help," by Samuel Smiles, has encouraged many young people in Japan. Mr. Leavitt's teaching and work as a missionary stirred up the spirit of self-support in the Church, and stamped this principle unconsciously upon many minds. Mr. Sawayama met the great need of the time by erecting this principle into a permanent power in Japan.

CHAPTER V.

WOMAN'S EDUCATION.

MR. SAWAYAMA was much interested in woman's education in Japan, and he contributed important ideas to the educational world. I wish to give my readers some idea of the education of Japanese women in order to show Mr. Sawayama's position.

The chief element of woman's education in old Japan was to cultivate what they called *jo-tokü* — woman's virtues. The first principles of jo-tokü were chastity and obedience. Thus the following sentiment has been familiar to Japanese women: "One woman should not know two men in her life." Therefore comparatively few women, especially in the upper class, ever married after losing their husbands. There were also a few instances where women lost their lives in defending their chastity.   As a rule, the morality of Japanese women was superior to that of the men.[1]

The most familiar sentiment in regard to the virtue of obedience was what they called *san-jiu* — the three obediences.   These three obediences were: first, to obey the parents in girlhood; second, to obey the husband in wifehood; third, to obey her oldest son after her husband's death.   So the woman's virtues were: to be obedient, meek, modest, humble, patient, temperate; to give the best to men; to give the upper seats to men; and to help her husband.

There existed the evil tendency of looking down upon women.   No doubt this custom was the result of the feudal system and the teachings of Confucianism and Buddhism.   As a rule, the Oriental idea was that "woman is as low as earth, while man is as high as heaven."

[1] There were many degraded girls in the lowest class, but in these instances men were more responsible than the girls themselves.

The next matter of importance in woman's training was etiquette, of which there were more than three thousand forms. It was regarded as an art of high order, hence the study of it by girls was insisted upon. The essential spirit of etiquette was the condition of mind; namely, tranquillity, peace in the heart, lovingkindness towards others, the spirit of self-sacrifice and self-denial, willingness to obey nature, and readiness to govern herself according to circumstances.

There were many forms and methods for doing things. For instance, there was a style of woman's writing which differed from man's way of expression.

The third important thing in a girl's education was sewing. The Japanese regarded the home as woman's sphere; so they thought sewing and housekeeping necessary things for girls to learn. This was the instruction for women: " Rise up early, sit up late, and do not take a nap in the daytime; give your attention to housekeeping, and be not lazy in sewing and weaving."

In addition to the training already mentioned, the parents of the samurai taught their daughters the art of fencing peculiar to women. The object was to produce the national spirit in the girls, so that when they became mothers they might inspire their children with an heroic spirit. It was also designed to make woman gracious and peaceful in her difficulties, and even before her enemies, as she trained herself to stand before them in defense. Thus the national spirit was developed to quite an extent among the women of the upper class.

There were several heroines who became famous by fighting in battle. In the history of Japan there were thirteen queens who really administered civil affairs, one of whom went to Korea to fight as a general. I could refer to many instances of heroines and those who had the strong national spirit among daughters of the samurai.

But even among another class of women we find the development of this same spirit. For instance, the daughter of a merchant committed suicide at the gate of the government building in Kyōtō in 1891, when Japan had some trouble. Her motive was self-sacrifice for her country's sake. As she was trained in the old Japanese way, her judgment was wrong, but her motive noble. She decided to die for her country, prepared for it, made a journey of two hundred miles to the gate, and committed harakiri calmly.

At the present time, a time of reformation in the country, especially in woman's sphere, the national spirit in young girls is very strong.

The greatest lack in woman's education was intellectual training. Higher education was thought to be unnecessary and impossible for women; so they only taught girls to read easy books, to write letters, and to know about those matters that pertained to woman's life and work in the household. Their education also included a knowledge of music and drawing, together with some poems. There were, however, exceptional cases. A few women acquired distinction as scholars and authors. When Japan opened her gates to Western civilization, she saw and admired the higher culture of women in other countries. As a result, the government adopted a school system, patterned after the best of other nations, and urged even girls from six years old to thirteen to attend the public schools.

Several scholars insisted upon woman's higher education. The missionaries of America were the first to start girls' schools for a higher education; and we are very much indebted to American lady missionaries for the progress of our women. But at that time there existed some feebleness and deficiencies in the schools, caused by the reliance of the native Christians upon foreign charity,

and also by the fact that the schools were
managed by missionaries who could not
appreciate fully Japanese needs.

Mr. Sawayama's school for girls was
the first self-supporting school, and set an
example which was followed by others
in due time. There are now quite a
number of self-supporting Christian girls'
schools. Even the mission schools are
changing ; for instance, one girls' school
in Tōkyō belonged to an American Missionary Society, and it was supported and
managed entirely by American ladies.
Japanese teachers were only their assist-
ants. But when Bishop William Hare
came to Japan in 1891 he saw the condition of things and judged it better to
let the Japanese support and manage their
own schools. So he executed a plan to re-
organize the school and to transfer the
power of management to the hands of
the Japanese.

The oldest and largest girls' school in
Osaka city is called the " Plum-blossom

Girls' School." If I explain the origin of the name, the reader may understand the origin of the school.

In 1878 there were only two small churches in Osaka city. One of them was called the Umemoto Church (meaning Plum-root Church), and the other, Naniwa Church (meaning Wave-blossom Church). The two churches contained about sixty members. They united to start a girls' school on a self-supporting basis. They raised about thirty dollars from the two churches. With this they rented a house and fitted up dormitories and class-rooms. Two of the founders were experienced teachers, and promised to manage the school and to teach in it almost without salary. They took the word " plum " from the name of one of the churches, and the word " blossom " from the name of the other, and called their school the Plum-blossom school.

The school was opened on the eleventh of January, 1878. It began with two

Japanese and two American teachers, and
fifteen pupils. It grew rapidly every
month; but after three months the house
which it was occupying was sold into other
hands. The school was obliged to move
into other quarters, and lost the thirty
dollars which it had invested.

The school labored under three special
difficulties: the people hated the Christian principles which were taught; public
opinion was opposed to the higher education of women; self-support was a great
task. Still it continued for two years,
when it became necessary to remove a
second time into new quarters. It seemed
almost impossible to support the school
any longer. But at this crisis all the
Christians encouraged the school authori-
ties, everybody contributed something, and
about five hundred dollars were collected.
With this the managers built a new
building, which was the property of the
school. The school has now two large
buildings which can accommodate more

than four hundred students. About six years ago the number of students increased to about four hundred. Just now there is a reaction in Japan against higher education for women, in consequence of which the number of pupils has decreased.[1] But I am sure that this will be but a temporary movement, and that the school will soon recover from it.

Fifteen years ago there was no high school for girls in Osaka city, which then contained a population of five hundred thousand. In the fourth year of the Plum-blossom School, Mr. Tateno, the governor of the province, who is now Japanese minister at Washington, paid the school a visit. He watched with especial admiration the experiments of the students in chemistry. He congratulated the girls upon their progress, and in

---

[1] At the most flourishing time of the school, the managers borrowed a large sum of money with which they built the large buildings. It was probably a great mistake, because when the reaction came they could not pay the debt and suffered a great deal. At last they secured temporary help from the American Board through the mission.

addressing the school he said that since
his whole province (containing a population of over 1,600,000) had but this one
high school for girls, he hoped the school
would prosper greatly. But now we have
many girls' high schools in Osaka city.

The Plum-blossom School teaches sciences, history, Japanese, Chinese, and
English literature, arithmetic, algebra,
geometry, music, sewing, domestic science,
etc. The school was modeled in some
respects after Mt. Holyoke Seminary. It
was animated by the same spirit of independence, economy, perseverance, and
service for others. So the pupils cooked,
swept, washed, and took care of the school-
rooms and the gardens. For many years
no servant was employed. Both teachers
and pupils worked very hard. The school
did not grow without many sacrifices and
struggles.

Mr. Sawayama, of course, was one of
the founders, and was for some time the
president of the Plum-blossom School.

He says in March, 1880 : " I began to conduct the daily religious exercises of our girls' school as I used to do before. We have over fifty girls and it is very interesting to help them to come to the Redeemer."

CHAPTER VI.

THE WORK IN NIIGATA.

HE province of Niigata is the northernmost and largest province of the main island of Japan. It contains a population of about 1,700,000. Niigata city is the capital of the province and a treaty port.

Eight years ago Dr. Palm, an English missionary, who had been working there earnestly for ten years, returned to his native land. The visible results of his work were small: for the people held fast to their faith in Buddhism. After Dr. Palm returned to England, Mr. O. H. Gulick, Mr. Davis, Dr. Doremus Scudder and his sister, took the field as missionaries of the American Board. Work was begun upon the self-supporting basis. Mr. Sawayama had preached in this field during the summer of 1884. He gave new life to the church. Two years later there came a crisis in the life of this Niigata church. The church had invited a preacher from Mr. Sawayama's church. From various circumstances he was hesitating, apparently unable to decide to go. Mr. Sawayama was very ill. He could hope to live only a very little while longer. The oft-repeated prophecy of his physicians could not remain much longer unfulfilled; but in his cheerful, courageous manner he persuaded his friend to leave him and go to the Niigata church.

In the early morning, when he was starting from Osaka, Mr. Sawayama, who at that time was not even allowed to see his friends in his own room, appeared at the station; and the last words which he spoke to his departing friend were not those of a weak or fainting spirit, but came from a heart alive as ever with Christian courage and good cheer. .

When the minister arrived at Niigata in 1886 there were only about twenty

Christians there; but the church increased
rapidly, and at the end of two years it contained about one hundred and fifty members. Two schools were also founded.

In this large province there had been
no girls' school, except a female department in the normal school. So a school
was founded upon the same basis as that
of the Plum-blossom School. The governor, the chief justice, the mayor, and
other leading citizens became trustees of
the school and helped it a great deal. In
two years this new school had two buildings worth $2,500, grounds worth $500,
and ninety scholars. The funds were
raised entirely from native contributions.

The prejudice of the people of Niigata
(especially of the older people) against
Christianity and the higher education of
women was much the same as that in
Osaka. One or two instances may illus-
trate the condition of affairs: —

A company of four girls, none of whom
were as yet Christians, lived in Nagaoka,

about thirty miles from Niigata. They became greatly dissatisfied with their lives and were carried away with the desire to receive a higher education. But they could not secure the permission of their parents. They often met and talked together, and in one of their secret conferences they agreed that it would be better to die than to live without making any progress.

One of them applied to an academy in the city for admission, but the reply fell into the hands of her father. Her father scolded her severely; her mother blamed her, and explained to her that there was no need of higher education for women. The girl made no remonstrance; but after the reproofs of her parents were finished she went to her room and committed suicide.

The next one of these four girls had a brother in Tōkyō University. When he returned to his home after graduation his sister begged him to take her with him to

Tōkyō to enter a girls' school; but he had no sympathy with her, and answered her that it would be better for her to stay at home and learn to cook and to sew. The poor girl was entirely discouraged; and when her brother left home for Tōkyō, she put an end to her life.

The parents of the third girl discovered the decision into which she had entered with her companions, and allowed her to enter the Normal School at Niigata.

The fourth girl became a Christian. But she was subjected to severe persecution by her parents, who at last sent her to a remote place where she could have no means of correspondence with any other Christians. Since that time nothing has been heard of her by her fellow Christians.

We heard of many cases in which girls wished to come to our schools, but their parents would not allow them to attend a school in which Christian principles were taught; but many girls overcame such obstacles and became students in them.

A gentleman wanted very much to send his daughter to our school in Niigata, but his old parents and his wife did not consent. He did not give up his hope, however. He attempted to overcome their prejudice. He began to read The Woman's Magazine and some books to his whole family every evening after supper. Thus he continued for six months to enlighten their darkened hearts. After six months of such work he was able to persuade his old parents and his wife to allow him to send his daughter to our school. I heard this story from his lips when he brought his daughter to Niigata.

It took another girl about two years to get her father's permission to enter our school. Having no hope of success, she formed another plan for improving herself. She organized a woman's club with her two older married sisters and some other girls in that town for mutual improvement. Her father then became so impressed with her strong aspiration for education that at length he permitted her to come to our school.

I will say only a word about the boys' school. The master of a private school was converted, and at once offered to turn his school into one in which Christian principles should be taught. A Christian gentleman contributed $2,000 and another gave $200. This was the beginning of the boys' school.

The self-sacrificing spirit of Dr. Henry Scudder and wife, and Miss Kendall, who came to Niigata to help the schools, they serving without salary, and in addition paying their own expenses, stimulated many Japanese to work for others without compensation, and also to contribute to these schools.

Mr. Sawayama's physical strength was almost exhausted. He lay in the hospital waiting for the last day. I called upon him, and in the course of conversation ventured to ask him if he did not feel lonesome. He answered very quickly but very quietly that he never did.

When he could no longer stand in his pulpit he began the compilation of a book of Christian biography. His saying that the day before his death he should do the same work as at any other time was no mere boast. Nor was there any element of bravado in the spirit with which he met death. He worked because just so long as he should remain in this world his life consisted in his work. When death came it found him not idly waiting. He had not finished his last task. His uncompleted manuscripts were gathered by his friends and published.

As death approached, Mr. Sawayama's mind was as clear as ever. He prepared to distribute the few possessions which he had among his friends. He wrote down the names, with the specification of the gift which he desired to give to each. His

inkstand he had planned to give to a
friend who lived at a considerable distance.
He found that the cover had been lost.
He ordered one to be made of silver. At
the last he called his little eight-year-old
daughter to his side. He gave her a gold
ring and spoke some words of encouragement to her. There was no longer occasion in his own life for that Christian
courage which had distinguished it from
the first; but as he left the world he
would communicate it to his child as his
best gift. He spoke to her about her
studies and her Christian life, and told her
to be patient till her uncle should return
from America to take care of her. He
died very peacefully and hopefully, March
27, 1887.

I have told his story with no attempt to
eulogize him, simply and plainly as it lies
in my own recollection. He was to me
and he is to my people a hero. So
bravely did he live and so bravely did he
die, that he might say with confidence

those great words of his great namesake ·
"I have fought a good fight, I have finished my course, I have kept the faith;
henceforth there is laid up for me a crown
of righteousness."

www.ingramcontent.com/pod-product-compliance
Lightning Source LLC
Chambersburg PA
CBHW022355020726
47500CB00002B/292